Saphira and Linus

**20 Kurzgeschichten
(Englisch / Deutsch) in Dialogform mit Übungen**

von

Bernhard Ludwig©

2. verbesserte Auflage

Bibliografische Information der Deutschen Nationalbibliothek: Die Deutsche Nationalbibliothek verzeichnet diese Publikation in der Deutschen Nationalbibliografie; detaillierte bibliografische Daten sind im Internet über dnb.dnb.de abrufbar.

©2022 Bernhard Ludwig
2. verbesserte Auflage 2024

Verlag: BoD · Books on Demand GmbH, In de Tarpen 42, 22848 Norderstedt

Druck: Libri Plureos GmbH, Friedensallee 273, 22763 Hamburg

ISBN: 978-3-7583-2925-8

Inhaltsverzeichnis

1 Saphira's Magic Performance

<Saphira and Linus are sitting in the living room. Saphira's magic performance will take place tomorrow. She's pretty nervous because it's her first time to perform her magic. Now Linus is trying to give her his advice even though he's not a wizard but a hamster warrior!>

Saphira: What spells should I use for the performance tomorrow?

<Linus is smiling>

Linus: Well, I guess you should use those spells which you are able to cast the best. Otherwise, it could happen that you singe a dwarf's beard or the skirt of a beautiful woman or ...

Saphira: Stop that, please! I've got more than enough spells that I'm able to cast without any problems ...

Linus: Why are you worried then?

Saphira: It's just … I want that the performance will be perfect! Everybody shall have fun and enjoy it!

1 Saphiras Zauberdarbietung

<Saphira und Linus sitzen gerade im Wohnzimmer. Saphiras Zauberaufführung wird morgen stattfinden. Sie ist ziemlich nervös, weil es ihr erstes Mal ist, ihre Magie darzubieten. Nun versucht Linus ihr seinen Rat zu geben, obwohl er kein Zauberer, sondern ein Hamsterkrieger ist!>

Saphira: Was für Zauber sollte ich für die morgige Darbietung verwenden?

<Linus lächelt>

Linus: Nun, ich schätze, du solltest die Zauber verwenden, die du am besten wirken kannst. Sonst könnte es passieren, dass du den Bart eines Zwergs ansengst oder den Rock einer schönen Frau oder ...

Saphira: Hör bitte damit auf! Ich habe genug Zauber, die ich ohne Probleme wirken kann ...

Linus: Warum machst du dir dann Sorgen?

Saphira: Es ist nur ... ich will, dass die Darbietung perfekt sein wird! Jeder soll Spaß haben und sich an ihr erfreuen!

Linus: I see … I've got an idea! You should not wear your magic robe but more trendy and sexy clothes!

<Saphira is blushing>

Saphira: Trendy and sexy?

Linus: Sure, but don't worry! I'll get you the right clothes for tomorrow!

<Linus is laughing>

Saphira: Oh dear ...

<Saphira's first magic performance will take place today>

Linus: Saphira! Come here and have a look, please! Your cool clothes for the performance are lying here ...

Saphira: A blue mini skirt with rose cat motifs … and a crop top?

<Linus is laughing>

Linus: Verstehe … Ich habe eine Idee! Du solltest nicht deine magische Robe, sondern eher modische und sexy Kleidung tragen!

<Saphira errötet>

Saphira: Modisch und sexy?

Linus: Sicher, aber mach dir keine Sorgen! Ich werde dir die richtige Kleidung für morgen besorgen!

<Linus lacht>

Saphira: Oje …

<Heute wird Saphiras Zauberdarbietung stattfinden>

Linus: Saphira! Bitte komm her und schau mal! Deine coole Kleidung für die Darbietung liegt hier …

Saphira: Ein blauer Minirock mit rosa Katzenmotiven … und ein bauchfreies Top?

<Linus lacht>

Linus: Yes! That's trendy and sexy! You'll be eye candy!

<Now Saphira is standing on the little stage to cast some spells for the people who have come to her performance>

A Dwarf: Wow! She's so beautiful!

Another Dwarf: Indeed! I'm looking forward to seeing her spells! If the spells are as beautiful as she is, I'm happy!

<Saphira is casting her first spell now>

Saphira: A blue fireball may appear!

<A blue fireball has appeared. It's moving in various directions>

Linus: I hope that she can cast every spell properly ...

<Now Saphira is casting her second spell>

Saphira: An imp may appear!

Linus: Ja! Das ist modisch und sexy! Du wirst ein Hingucker sein!

<Nun steht Saphira auf der kleinen Bühne, um ein paar Zauber für die Leute, die zur Darbietung gekommen sind, zu wirken>

Ein Zwerg: Wow! Sie ist so schön!

Ein anderer Zwerg: In der Tat! Ich freue mich darauf, ihre Zauber zu sehen! Wenn die Zauber so schön sind wie sie, bin ich glücklich!

<Saphira wirkt nun ihren ersten Zauber>

Saphira: Ein blauer Feuerball möge erscheinen!

<Ein blauer Feuerball ist erschienen. Er bewegt sich in verschiedene Richtungen>

Linus: Ich hoffe, dass sie jeden Zauber richtig wirken kann ...

<Nun wirkt Saphira ihren zweiten Zauber>

Saphira: Ein Kobold möge erscheinen!

<Suddenly, a little imp has appeared. It's jumping around the stage and pulling faces. The people are laughing. A few minutes have passed. The imp has disappeared. Two hours later ...>

Linus: It's been a fantastic performance, Saphira! I'm impressed!

Saphira: Thank you, Linus! I'm so happy that everything worked fine!

<Saphira and Linus are laughing>

<Plötzlich ist ein kleiner Kobold erschienen. Er springt auf der Bühne umher und schneidet Grimassen. Die Leute lachen. Ein paar Minuten sind vergangen. Der Kobold ist verschwunden. Zwei Stunden später ...>

Linus: Das ist eine fantastische Darbietung gewesen, Saphira! Ich bin beeindruckt!

Saphira: Danke, Linus! Ich bin glücklich, dass alles gut funktioniert hat!

<Saphira und Linus lachen>

2 Attack of Some Bloodthirsty Dragons

<Saphira and Linus are having breakfast while sitting in the garden. It's a sunny day in July>

Saphira: Isn't the weather nice today?

Linus: Yes, it is! But I'm a bit sweating … I've got fur, you know …

<Saphira is laughing>

Saphira: Well, maybe I should shave it off?

Linus: I don't think that this would be a good idea … I can't walk around naked!

<Behold! The sky is getting dark>

Saphira: What is happening?

Linus: I don't know … Oh no! Look, there are dragons!

Saphira: We must drive them out of here!

Linus: Yes! I'll get my mighty warhammer!

2 Angriff einiger blutrünstiger Drachen

<Saphira und Linus frühstücken gerade, während sie im Garten sitzen. Es ist ein sonniger Tag im Juli>

Saphira: Ist das Wetter heute nicht schön?

Linus: Ja, ist es! Aber ich schwitze ein wenig … Ich habe Fell, wie du weißt …

<Saphira lacht>

Saphira: Nun, vielleicht sollte ich es abrasieren?

Linus: Ich glaube nicht, dass das eine gute Idee wäre … Ich kann nicht nackt herumlaufen!

<Siehe! Der Himmel verdunkelt sich>

Saphira: Was geschieht?

Linus: Ich weiß es nicht … Oh nein! Schau, dort sind Drachen!

Saphira: Wir müssen sie von hier vertreiben!

Linus: Ja! Ich hole meinen mächtigen Kriegshammer!

<The dragons are attacking the town guard and destroying houses>

Saphira: Well, I'm not a fully educated wizard yet, but I'll do my best to fight them!

Linus: Here we are, you damn, stinky dragons!

<Now the dragons are flying towards Linus>

Saphira: Are you crazy?!

Linus: Don't be afraid! I'm going to send them to hell!

<Linus is laughing while brandishing his warhammer, and Saphira is casting a spell to dazzle the dragons>

Linus: That's great, Saphira!

<Now Linus is hitting all dragons with his warhammer while turning somersaults>

Saphira: That's amazing, Linus!

<Die Drachen greifen gerade die Stadtwache an und zerstören Häuser>

Saphira: Nun, ich bin noch keine komplett ausgebildete Zauberin, aber ich werde mein Bestes geben, sie zu bekämpfen!

Linus: Hier sind wir, ihr verdammten, stinkenden Drachen!

<Jetzt fliegen die Drachen auf Linus zu>

Saphira: Bist du verrückt?!

Linus: Habe keine Angst! Ich werde sie in die Hölle schicken!

<Linus lacht, während er seinen Kriegshammer schwingt, und Saphira wirkt einen Zauber, um die Drachen zu blenden>

Linus: Das ist großartig, Saphira!

<Nun schlägt Linus alle Drachen mit seinem Kriegshammer, während er Salti macht>

Saphira: Das ist beeindruckend, Linus!

<Linus is laughing>

Saphira: Now I'll throw a fireball against the dragons!

<Saphira and Linus are fighting the dragons very bravely>

Linus: I think that we should have put them to flight very soon!

Saphira: Yes, I think so, too!

<A black dragon has just hit Linus with his tail, and Linus is being catapulted into the air now>

Linus: Damn! This stinky dragon – hey, now I'm learning how to fly!

<Linus is laughing>

Saphira: Linus!

<Saphira is very angry now. She's feeling a power that she hasn't felt ever before>

<Linus lacht>

Saphira: Nun werde ich einen Feuerball gegen die Drachen schleudern!

<Saphira und Linus bekämpfen die Drachen sehr tapfer>

Linus: Ich denke, dass wir sie sehr bald in die Flucht geschlagen haben sollten!

Saphira: Ja, das denke ich auch!

<Ein schwarzer Drache hat gerade Linus mit seinem Schwanz getroffen und Linus wird nun in die Luft katapultiert>

Linus: Verdammt! Dieser stinkende Drache – hey, nun lerne ich, wie man fliegt!

<Linus lacht>

Saphira: Linus!

<Saphira ist nun sehr wütend. Sie spürt eine Kraft, die sie noch nie zuvor gespürt hat>

Saphira: Wow, what's this power?!

<Saphira has just cast a spell, and now many lightnings are striking the dragons>

Saphira: Cool!

<Behold! The dragons are screaming while flying away>

Saphira: Wow, was ist das für eine Kraft?!

<Saphira hat gerade einen Zauber gewirkt und nun schlagen viele Blitze in die Drachen ein>

Saphira: Cool!

<Siehe! Die Drachen schreien, während sie davon fliegen>

3 The Sad Dwarf and the Golem

<Saphira and Linus are walking along a stream. Now they're hearing somebody crying ...>

Saphira: Do you hear that?

Linus: Yes, it sounds like a crying dwarf ... Dwarfs don't cry often, so it must be something serious.

Saphira: The crying voice seems to come from the mine ...

<Linus stops walking and is listening very carefully now ...>

Linus: Yes, you're right. Let's go there!

<Saphira is nodding>

Saphira: There's the crying dwarf! He's sitting on a small rock next to the entrance of the mine.

Linus: Hey, what's the matter, my friend?

3 Der traurige Zwerg und der Golem

<Saphira und Linus laufen gerade an einem Fluss entlang. Jetzt hören sie jemanden weinen ...>

Saphira: Hörst du das?

Linus: Ja, es hört sich wie ein weinender Zwerg an ... Zwerge weinen nicht oft, also muss es etwas Ernstes sein.

Saphira: Die weinerliche Stimme scheint von der Mine zu kommen ...

<Linus hört auf zu gehen und hört nun sehr genau hin ...>

Linus: Ja, du hast recht. Lass uns dorthin gehen!

<Saphira nickt>

Saphira: Dort ist der weinende Zwerg! Er sitzt auf einem kleinen Felsen neben dem Mineneingang.

Linus: Hey, was ist los, mein Freund?

Dwarf: I've lost my beloved pickaxe!

<The dwarf is crying loudly>

Saphira: Your pickaxe?!

Dwarf: Yes, I got it for my first birthday! We used to do everything together!

Saphira: It seems that you really like your pickaxe ...

Linus: Sure, it's obvious that he loves it; why not? I used to wear a special pair of briefs when I was young. I really loved it! Unfortunately, some day an orc stole it while I was having a bath ...

<Saphira is shaking her head while smiling>

Saphira: Well ... I think we should try to get your pickaxe back ...

Dwarf: That's not so easy ...

Zwerg: Ich habe meine geliebte Spitzhacke verloren!

<Der Zwerg weint laut>

Saphira: Deine Spitzhacke?!

Zwerg: Ja, ich habe sie zu meinem ersten Geburtstag bekommen! Wir machten damals alles zusammen!

Saphira: Es scheint, dass du deine Spitzhacke sehr gerne hast ...

Linus: Sicher, es ist offensichtlich, dass er sie liebt; warum nicht? Ich trug damals eine besondere Unterhose. Ich liebte sie sehr! Unglücklicherweise stahl sie ein Ork, während ich ein Bad nahm ...

<Saphira schüttelt ihren Kopf, während sie lächelt>

Saphira: Nun ... ich denke, wir sollten versuchen, deine Spitzhacke zurückzuholen ...

Zwerg: Das ist nicht so einfach ...

Linus: What do you mean?

Dwarf: I was working in the mine when suddenly a golem appeared, pushed me over, took my beloved pickaxe, and ran away!

Saphira: Oh dear ...

Linus: Don't worry, my fat friend! Saphira and I'll go into the mine and get your pickaxe!

Dwarf: Really? Thank you so much! I'll be waiting here.

<Saphira and Linus have entered the mine>

Saphira: Well, where could that golem have gone?

Linus: Probably that golem hates mineworkers ... I think we should start working!

Saphira: Well, that could work ... Ok, let's do it!

Linus: Was meinst du?

Zwerg: Ich arbeitete in der Mine, als plötzlich ein Golem auftauchte, mich zu Boden warf, meine geliebte Spitzhacke nahm und davonrannte!

Saphira: Oje ...

Linus: Mach dir keine Sorgen, mein dicker Freund! Saphira und ich werden in die Mine gehen und deine Spitzhacke holen!

Zwerg: Wirklich? Ich danke euch so sehr! Ich werde hier warten.

<Saphira und Linus haben die Mine betreten>

Saphira: Also, wo könnte jener Golem hingegangen sein?

Linus: Wahrscheinlich hasst der Golem Minenarbeiter ... Ich denke, wir sollten anfangen zu arbeiten!

Saphira: Nun, das könnte funktionieren ... Ok, machen wir es!

<Only a few minutes later, the golem has appeared, holding the pickaxe in his hands>

Linus: Give us the pickaxe!

<While the golem is running towards Linus, it's brandishing the pickaxe>

Saphira: Don't worry, I can cast a good spell!

<A strong gust of wind has pushed the golem into a deep hole>

Linus: Cool, he's disappeared.

Saphira: Yes, I think he won't be able to do something stupid for some time. Let's take the pickaxe and go to the dwarf.

Linus: I'll do that.

<Saphira and Linus have just come out of the mine>

Dwarf: My beloved pickaxe!

<Now the dwarf is running to Linus>

<Nach nur wenigen Minuten ist der Golem, die Spitzhacke in seinen Händen haltend, erschienen>

Linus: Gib uns die Spitzhacke!

<Während der Golem auf Linus zurennt, schwingt er die Spitzhacke>

Saphira: Keine Sorge, ich kann einen guten Zauber wirken!

<Eine starke Windböe hat den Golem in ein tiefes Loch gestoßen>

Linus: Cool, er ist verschwunden!

Saphira: Ja, ich denke, er wird für eine Weile keine Dummheiten mehr machen können. Lass uns die Spitzhacke nehmen und zum Zwerg gehen.

Linus: Das mache ich.

<Saphira und Linus sind gerade aus der Mine gekommen>

Zwerg: Meine geliebte Spitzhacke!

<Nun rennt der Zwerg zu Linus>

4 Saphira and the Jewel of the Sun

<Saphira and Linus are working in the garden>

A Dwarf: We've found a wonderful jewel in the mine! It's … eh … wonderful as I said!

A Woman: Wow! It's sparkling and glowing! You should show it to the Queen.

A Dwarf: Alright, I'll do that!

Saphira: A sparkling and glowing jewel?

Linus: That's the right thing for a woman!

Saphira: Come on, let's follow the dwarf and have a look at the jewel.

Linus: No, I don't feel like doing that right now. I'm going to take a nap in the hammock.

<Saphira is rolling her eyes>

Saphira: Alright, then I'll just go by myself! Bye!

4 Saphira und das Juwel der Sonne

<Saphira und Linus arbeiten gerade im Garten>

Ein Zwerg: Wir haben ein wundervolles Juwel in der Mine gefunden! Es ist … äh … wundervoll, wie ich gesagt habe!

Eine Frau: Wow! Es funkelt und leuchtet! Du solltest es der Königin zeigen.

Ein Zwerg: Alles klar, das mache ich!

Saphira: Ein funkelndes und leuchtendes Juwel?

Linus: Das ist das Richtige für eine Frau!

Saphira: Komm schon, lass uns dem Zwerg folgen und einen Blick auf das Juwel werfen.

Linus: Nein, ich habe jetzt keine Lust darauf. Ich werde ein Nickerchen in der Hängematte machen.

<Saphira verdreht die Augen>

Saphira: Alles klar, dann gehe ich eben alleine! Tschüss!

Linus: Bye-bye!

<Saphira has followed the dwarf, and now she is in front of the Queen's palace>

Saphira: Ah, that is … the jewel ... Hm, it looks like a jewel which I saw some years ago in an old book. I should go to the library and have a look at the book again.

<Now Saphira is sitting in the library reading the old book>

Saphira: Here it is … Oh dear! This jewel is called 'The Jewel of the Sun' ... It's pretty dangerous because if somebody throws it against something, or it falls down by accident, it explodes! I must tell that the Queen immediately!

<Saphira is hearing a loud explosion>

Saphira: Oh no!

Linus: Saphira! There's just been an explosion in the palace of the Queen!

Linus: Tschüss!

<Saphira ist dem Zwerg gefolgt und nun ist sie vor dem Palast der Königin>

Saphira: Ah, das ist … das Juwel … Hm, es sieht wie ein Juwel aus, das ich vor ein paar Jahren in einem alten Buch gesehen habe. Ich sollte zur Bibliothek gehen und nochmal einen Blick in das Buch werfen.

<Nun sitzt Saphira, das Buch lesend, in der Bibliothek>

Saphira: Hier ist es … Oje! Dieses Juwel wird „Juwel der Sonne" genannt … Es ist ziemlich gefährlich, weil, wenn jemand es gegen etwas wirft oder es aus Versehen hinunterfällt, explodiert es! Ich muss das sofort der Königin sagen!

<Saphira hört eine laute Explosion>

Saphira: Oh nein!

Linus: Saphira! Es hat gerade eine Explosion im Palast der Königin gegeben!

Saphira: Let's go there at once!

<A few minutes have passed. Saphira and Linus have reached the palace>

Linus: What a mess!

<Half of the palace is destroyed>

A Town Guard: Don't worry, good people! Nobody is injured! Please go home now!

Linus: Hm, it seems that everybody is ok ...

Saphira: Let's go home. I think I know what has happened. I'll tell you as soon as we've arrived home.

Linus: Sounds good!

<Saphira has just told Linus about the Jewel of the Sun>

Linus: Ah, I see. Probably, the dwarf dropped it when he wanted to give it to the Queen.

Saphira: Lass uns sofort dorthin gehen!

<Ein paar Minuten sind vergangen. Saphira und Linus haben den Palast erreicht>

Linus: Was für ein Chaos!

<Der halbe Palast ist zerstört>

Eine Stadtwache: Keine Sorge, gute Bürger! Niemand ist verletzt! Bitte geht nun nach Hause!

Linus: Hm, es scheint, dass jeder ok ist ...

Saphira: Lass uns nach Hause gehen. Ich denke, ich weiß, was geschehen ist. Ich werde es dir sagen, sobald wir zu Hause angekommen sind.

Linus: Hört sich gut an!

<Saphira hat Linus gerade vom Juwel der Sonne erzählt>

Linus: Ah, verstehe. Wahrscheinlich ließ der Zwerg das Juwel fallen, als er es der Königin geben wollte.

Saphira: This could have happened. I think we should go to the Queen tomorrow and tell her what kind of jewel it was.

Linus: Ok!

<Saphira and Linus have just told the Queen about the Jewel of the Sun>

Queen: Yes, the dwarf dropped it when he wanted to give me the jewel.

Linus: You see, Saphira.

Queen: Fortunately, I was able to protect everybody who was in the palace with my magic ring.

Linus: Wow! That's cool!

Queen: I've already sent out a herold to tell the dwarfs not to search for more of these jewels.

Saphira: Ah, that's good! What a relief!

Saphira: Das könnte geschehen sein. Ich denke, wir sollten morgen zur Königin gehen und ihr sagen, was für eine Art von Juwel es war.

Linus: Ok!

<Saphira und Linus haben der Königin gerade vom Juwel der Sonne erzählt>

Königin: Ja, der Zwerg ließ es fallen, als er mir das Juwel geben wollte.

Linus: Siehst du, Saphira.

Königin: Glücklicherweise war es mir möglich, jeden, der im Palast war, mit meinem magischen Ring zu schützen.

Linus: Wow! Das ist cool!

Königin: Ich habe bereits einen Boten entsandt, um den Zwergen mitzuteilen, nicht nach weiteren Juwelen zu suchen.

Saphira: Ah, das ist gut! Was für eine Erleichterung!

Queen: I thank you so much for coming to me, Saphira and Linus! You'll receive a present shortly.

Saphira: We are honoured! Thank you!

Linus: Indeed, thank you!

Königin: Ich danke euch so sehr, dass ihr zu mir gekommen seid, Saphira und Linus! Ihr werdet in Kürze ein Geschenk erhalten!

Saphira: Wir fühlen uns geehrt! Danke!

Linus: In der Tat, danke!

5 The Ghost of the Lake?!

<Saphira is going for a walk in the forest>

Saphira: It's a beautiful night! The stars are sparkling, and it's quite warm – wait … What's that? A strange sound is coming from the lake over there.

<Saphira is running to the lake now>

Saphira: It's pretty foggy here ...

Voice: Who are you?

<Saphira is a bit scared>

Saphira: Is there anybody?

Voice: I'm here … in the lake ...

Saphira: In the lake? How are you able to speak?

Voice: I'm dead ...

Saphira: Dead?! You're a ghost?!

5 Der Geist des Sees?!

<Saphira geht gerade im Wald spazieren>

Saphira: Es ist eine schöne Nacht! Die Sterne funkeln und es ist recht warm – warte … Was ist das? Ein seltsames Geräusch kommt vom See dort drüben.

<Saphira rennt nun zum See>

Saphira: Es ist ziemlich neblig hier …

Stimme: Wer bist du?

<Saphira hat ein wenig Angst>

Saphira: Ist dort jemand?

Stimme: Ich bin hier … im See ...

Saphira: Im See? Wie ist es dir möglich, zu sprechen?

Stimme: Ich bin tot ...

Saphira: Tot?! Du bist ein Geist?!

Voice: Don't be afraid … I won't hurt you. I'm so lonely. I can't rest in peace because I wasn't able to say goodbye to my dear ones ...

Saphira: I could help you – I could try to find your family and bring them to you.

Voice: Really? You would do this for me?

Saphira: Sure, please tell me their names and where they live.

Voice: Their names are Lydia, my wife, and Ayleen, my daughter. They should still live in town.

Saphira: All right, as soon as I've found them, I'll bring them to you at night, ok?

Voice: Thank you!

\<Saphira has just come back home\>

Stimme: Hab keine Angst … Ich werde dir nicht wehtun. Ich bin so einsam. Ich kann nicht in Frieden ruhen, weil es mir nicht möglich war, mich von ihnen zu verabschieden …

Saphira: Ich könnte dir helfen – ich könnte versuchen, deine Familie zu finden und sie zu dir bringen.

Stimme: Wirklich? Das würdest du für mich tun?

Saphira: Sicher, bitte sage mir ihre Namen und wo sie wohnen.

Stimme: Ihre Namen sind Lydia, meine Frau, und Ayleen, meine Tochter. Sie sollten noch immer in der Stadt leben.

Saphira: Alles klar. Sobald ich sie gefunden habe, werde ich sie in der Nacht zu dir bringen, ok?

Stimme: Danke!

<Saphira ist gerade nach Hause zurückgekehrt>

Linus: You've been for a walk quite long … What have you been doing?

\<Saphira has just told Linus about the things that happened\>

Linus: Are you sure that you're feeling well?

Saphira: I do not lie! Everything I've just told you is true, believe me!

Linus: Ok, ok, I believe you! Let's search the two in the morning.

\<Saphira and Linus are in town\>

Saphira: Let's ask the people in the local inn.

Linus: Sounds good – I'm starving ...

Saphira: We go there to ask the people if they know where we can find Lydia and Ayleen and not to have breakfast!

\<Linus sighs\>

Linus: Du bist recht lange spazieren gegangen … Was hast du getrieben?

<Saphira hat Linus gerade von den Dingen, die geschehen sind, erzählt>

Linus: Bist du sicher, dass es dir gut geht?

Saphira: Ich lüge nicht! Alles, was ich dir gerade erzählt habe, ist wahr, glaube mir!

Linus: Ok, ok, ich glaube dir! Lass uns die beiden am Morgen suchen.

<Saphira und Linus sind in der Stadt>

Saphira: Lass uns die Leute in der hiesigen Gaststätte fragen.

Linus: Hört sich gut an – ich verhungere ...

Saphira: Wir gehen dorthin, um die Leute zu fragen, ob sie wissen, wo wir Lydia und Ayleen finden können, und nicht, um zu frühstücken!

<Linus seufzt>

Linus: All right ...

<They're asking an old man now ...>

Saphira: Do you know a woman named Lydia and her daughter Ayleen?

Old Man: Yes, I know them. They live at a farm to the west of this town.

Linus: Thank you! Have a nice day!

Saphira: Ok, Linus, let's go there!

<Half an hour later ...>

Linus: Over there's the farm!

Saphira: Hello? Is anybody here?

Ayleen: Hello! Yes, I live here with my mum. She's working on the field at the moment.

<Now Saphira is telling her what her dead father told her>

Ayleen: I believe you; that sounds like dad ... Please wait here for a moment; I'll bring my mum here.

Linus: Alles klar ...

<Sie fragen nun einen alten Mann ...>

Saphira: Kennst du eine Frau namens Lydia und ihre Tochter Ayleen?

Alter Mann: Ja, ich kenne sie. Sie leben auf einem Bauernhof westlich der Stadt.

Linus: Danke! Habe einen schönen Tag!

Saphira: Ok, Linus, lass uns dorthin gehen!

<Eine halbe Stunde später ...>

Linus: Dort vorne ist der Bauernhof!

Saphira: Hallo? Ist jemand hier?

Ayleen: Hallo! Ja, ich lebe hier mit meiner Mama. Sie arbeitet gerade auf dem Feld.

<Nun teilt Saphira ihr mit, was ihr Vater ihr gesagt hat>

Ayleen: Ich glaube dir, das klingt nach Papa ... Bitte wartet hier einen Moment, ich bringe meine Mama her.

Linus: Ok!

<A few minutes have passed. Saphira, Linus, Ayleen, and Lydia are going to Saphira and Linus' house>

Saphira: Let's wait here until it's night.

Lydia: I can't wait to see him again ...

Saphira: Well, I'm sorry, but I don't think that you'll see him. While I was talking with him, I was hearing his voice but wasn't seeing him.

Lydia: Oh, I see.

<A few hours later ...>

Linus: Well, ladies ... I think it's time to go to the lake now.

Saphira: Yes, you're right.

<A few minutes have passed. They are all standing in front of the lake>

Linus: Ok!

<Ein paar Minuten sind vergangen. Saphira, Linus, Ayleen und Lydia gehen gerade zu Saphira und Linus' Haus>

Saphira: Lasst uns hier warten, bis es Nacht ist.

Lydia: Ich kann es nicht erwarten, ihn wiederzusehen ...

Saphira: Nun, es tut mir leid, aber ich glaube nicht, dass du ihn sehen wirst. Während ich mit ihm sprach, hörte ich seine Stimme, aber sah ihn nicht.

Lydia: Oh, verstehe.

<Ein paar Stunden später ...>

Linus: Nun, meine Damen ... ich denke, es ist nun Zeit, zum See zu gehen.

Saphira: Ja, du hast recht.

<Ein paar Minuten sind vergangen. Sie alle stehen vor dem See>

Voice: Lydia, Ayleen!

Lydia: Kane!

Ayleen: Daddy!

Kane: Yes, my dear ones! I'm here ... I can't rest in peace because I had no chance to say goodbye to you ...

Lydia: We miss you so much!

Kane: I know, but there's no way to get my life back …
So ... I want to say that I love you, Lydia and Ayleen, and that I'll be waiting for you in the hereafter. We'll see each other someday ... Farewell!

<The voice has disappeared. Lydia and Ayleen are crying, while Saphira and Linus are trying to console them>

Stimme: Lydia, Ayleen!

Lydia: Kane!

Ayleen: Vati!

Kane: Ja, meine Lieben! Ich bin hier …Ich kann nicht in Frieden ruhen, weil ich keine Gelegenheit hatte, mich von euch zu verabschieden …

Lydia: Wir vermissen dich so sehr!

Kane: Ich weiß, aber es gibt keine Möglichkeit, mein Leben zurückzubekommen … Also … ich will euch sagen, dass ich euch liebe, Lydia und Ayleen, und dass ich auf euch im Jenseits warten werde. Wir werden uns eines Tages wiedersehen … Lebt wohl!

<Die Stimme ist verschwunden. Lyida und Ayleen weinen, während Saphira und Linus versuchen sie zu trösten>

6 The Medicine for the Queen of the Elves

Linus: Saphira?

Saphira: Oh, you're back from shopping. Have you bought the cookbook?

Linus: Of course, here you are.

Saphira: Thank you, Linus! I'll cook something special for us for dinner!

Linus: I love sweet things … Maybe you could keep this in mind when you decide the dish.

Saphira: Yes, of course, I'll do that.

Linus: The people say that the Queen of the Elves is ill ...

Saphira: Oh dear! I hope that it's nothing serious.

Linus: I don't know ...

Saphira: I've got an idea! Let's cook something for her and after that I'll teleport it to her!

6 Die Medizin für die Königin der Elfen

Linus: Saphira?

Saphira: Oh, du bist vom Einkaufen zurück! Hast du das Kochbuch gekauft?

Linus: Selbstverständlich, hier.

Saphira: Danke, Linus! Ich werde etwas Besonderes für uns zum Abendessen kochen!

Linus: Ich liebe süße Dinge … Vielleicht könntest du das berücksichtigen, wenn du das Gericht auswählst.

Saphira: Ja, selbstverständlich, das werde ich tun.

Linus: Die Leute sagen, dass die Königin der Elfen krank sei …

Saphira: Oje! Ich hoffe, es ist nichts Ernstes.

Linus: Ich weiß es nicht …

Saphira: Ich habe eine Idee! Lass uns ihr etwas kochen und danach werde ich es zu ihr teleportieren!

Linus: Are you sure that you're able to teleport it?

Saphira: Yes, I've never tried it before, but I'm pretty sure that it'll work!

Linus: Hopefully, you won't teleport me to a dragon refuge or something like that by mistake ...

<Saphira is laughing>

Saphira: Trust me! It'll work!

<Now Saphira and Linus are cooking a delicious soup for the Queen of the Elves>

Linus: Let me taste it, please!

Saphira: No! Keep your dirty paws out of the soup!

Linus: Dirty?! I'm clean and good-smelling!

<Saphira is laughing>

Linus: Bist du sicher, dass du dazu fähig bist, es zu teleportieren?

Saphira: Ja, ich habe es noch nie zuvor ausprobiert, aber ich bin mir ziemlich sicher, dass es funktionieren wird!

Linus: Hoffentlich wirst du mich nicht aus Versehen in einen Drachenhort oder so etwas in der Art teleportieren ...

<Saphira lacht>

Saphira: Vertrau mir! Es wird funktionieren!

<Nun kochen Saphira und Linus eine köstliche Suppe für die Königin der Elfen>

Linus: Lass sie mich mal probieren, bitte!

Saphira: Nein! Nimm deine dreckigen Pfoten aus der Suppe!

Linus: Dreckig?! Ich bin sauber und rieche gut!

<Saphira lacht>

Saphira: So, the soup is ready to be teleported!

Linus: Oh dear ...

Saphira: Here we go!

<Saphira is casting a spell now>

Linus: Well, the soup is gone, but we don't know if the Queen of the Elves has received it.

Saphira: No problem! We only need to look in this crystal ball.

Linus: I can't see anything ...

<Saphira is smiling>

Saphira: I need to cast a spell first.

<Saphira has just cast a spell>

Linus: Now I can see her lying on her bed ... Oh, don't look!

Saphira: Why?

Saphira: So, die Suppe ist bereit, teleportiert zu werden!

Linus: Oje ...

Saphira: Los geht's!

<Saphira wirkt nun einen Zauber>

Linus: Nun, die Suppe ist fort, aber wir wissen nicht, ob die Königin der Elfen sie erhalten hat.

Saphira: Kein Problem! Wir müssen nur in diese Kristallkugel schauen.

Linus: Ich kann nichts sehen ...

<Saphira lächelt>

Saphira: Ich muss zuerst einen Zauber wirken.

<Saphira hat soeben den Zauber gewirkt>

Linus: Nun kann ich sie in ihrem Bett liegen sehen ... Oh, schaue nicht!

Saphira: Warum?

<Linus is whispering>

Linus: She's naked ...

<Saphira is laughing>

Saphira: Have you forgotten that I'm a girl, too? YOU are not allowed to look at her in this condition because your a male!

<Saphira grabs the crystal ball out of Linus' pawns>

Linus: Hey!

Saphira: Yes! She's received the soup! She's even eating it!

Queen of the Elves: Well, I don't know who's teleported this delicious soup to me, but I'm very grateful! I'm feeling better now ... Probably this is a medicine! I don't know who you are ... but thank you!

Saphira: Have you heard?

Linus: Of course, I'm not deaf!

<Linus flüstert>

Linus: Sie ist nackt ...

<Saphira lacht>

Saphira: Hast du vergessen, dass ich auch ein Mädchen bin? DIR ist es nicht erlaubt, sie in diesem Zustand anzuschauen, weil du ein Männchen bist!

<Saphira reißt Linus die Kristallkugel aus den Pfoten>

Linus: Hey!

Saphira: Ja! Sie hat die Suppe erhalten! Sie isst sie sogar!

Königin der Elfen: Nun, ich weiß nicht, wer diese köstliche Suppe zu mir teleportiert hat, aber ich bin sehr dankbar! Ich fühle mich jetzt besser ... Wahrscheinlich ist es eine Medizin! Ich weiß nicht, wer du bist ... aber danke!

Saphira: Hast du gehört?

Linus: Selbstverständlich, ich bin nicht taub!

Saphira: Ah, she's fallen asleep. I think I should end the spell now.

Linus: Oh, it's already time for dinner! You've forgotten to cook something delicious for us!

Saphira: Don't worry. Let's just cook the soup again!

Linus: Ok, that's fine!

<Saphira and Linus are laughing>

Saphira: Ah, sie ist eingeschlafen. Ich denke, ich sollte den Zauber nun beenden.

Linus: Oh, es ist schon Zeit für das Abendessen! Du hast vergessen, etwas Köstliches für uns zu kochen!

Saphira: Keine Sorge. Lass uns einfach nochmal die Suppe kochen!

Linus: Ok, das ist in Ordnung!

<Saphira und Linus lachen>

7 The Dwarves' Wild Feast

<It's a stormy night in August. Saphira is learning a new spell, while Linus is sleeping in his little hammock. Now a dwarf is knocking on the door ...>

Saphira: That's strange ... Why would somebody visit us at night?

<Saphira has just opened the door>

Dwarf: I'm sorry to disturb you, but I'd like to invite Linus and you to my feast tomorrow evening.

Saphira: A feast?

Dwarf: Yes, it's a feast to thank the God of Mining for protecting us.

Saphira: Ah, I see. All right, we'll come! I'm looking forward to it. I'm pretty sure that Linus will be happy about your invitation, too. Unfortunately, he's sleeping at the moment ...

<The dwarf is laughing>

7 Der Zwerge wildes Fest

<Es ist eine stürmische Nacht im August. Saphira lernt gerade einen neuen Zauber, während Linus in seiner kleinen Hängematte schläft. Nun klopft ein Zwerg an die Tür ...>

Saphira: Das ist komisch ... Warum sollte uns jemand in der Nacht besuchen?

<Saphira hat gerade die Tür geöffnet>

Zwerg: Es tut mir leid, euch zu stören, aber ich möchte Linus und dich zu meinem Fest morgen Abend einladen.

Saphira: Ein Fest?

Zwerg: Ja, es ist ein Fest, um dem Gott des Bergbaus dafür zu danken, dass er uns beschützt.

Saphira: Ah, verstehe. Alles klar, wir kommen! Ich freue mich darauf! Ich bin mir ziemlich sicher, dass auch Linus sich über deine Einladung freuen wird. Unglücklicherweise schläft er gerade ...

<Der Zwerg lacht>

Dwarf: No problem! It's night, so people should be sleeping now. I've worked too long in the mine; that's the reason why I've come here so late. Ok, then I'll see you tomorrow at the 'Ginrenok Estate'.

<Saphira is smiling>

Saphira: Perfect! Have a good night! Bye!

Dwarf: Thank you! Bye!

<One day has passed. Saphira and Linus are on the way to the Ginrenok Estate>

Linus: I love feasts! I hope that there's enough for me to eat and drink!

Saphira: Certainly! There should be enough for everyone ...

<Linus is laughing while climbing up to Saphira's right shoulder>

Linus: We'll see ...

Zwerg: Kein Problem! Es ist Nacht, also sollten die Leute nun schlafen. Ich habe zu lange in der Mine gearbeitet, das ist der Grund, warum ich so spät hierhergekommen bin. Ok, ich sehe euch dann morgen auf dem „Ginrenok Landgut".

<Saphira lächelt>

Saphira: Perfekt! Habe eine gute Nacht! Tschüss!

Zwerg: Danke! Tschüss!

<Ein Tag ist vergangen. Saphira und Linus sind auf dem Weg zum Ginrenok Landgut>

Linus: Ich liebe Feste! Ich hoffe, es gibt genug für mich zu essen und zu trinken!

Saphira: Sicherlich! Es sollte genug für jedermann geben ...

<Linus lacht, während er auf Saphiras rechte Schulter klettert>

Linus: Wir werden sehen ...

<An hour has passed. Saphira and Linus have just arrived at the estate. There are a lot of people; some are dancing and singing, some are talking to each other, and some are participating in various competitions>

Linus: Here we go!

<Behold! Linus is running towards a table with many delicious cakes>

Saphira: Oh dear … Linus will definitely overdo it again …

Dwarf: It's time to praise the God of Mining! Please raise your tankards! Hip, hip, hurray!

<All dwarfs are finishing their drink. Linus stops eating and scratches himself behind his left ear. A few seconds have passed. Linus continues eating>

Dwarf: Thank you, everyone! Enjoy yourselves!

<A dwarf with a beautiful hat has just fallen into the river, which goes along the estate. Saphira is running to him …>

<Eine Stunde ist vergangen. Saphira und Linus sind gerade auf dem Landgut angekommen. Es sind viele Leute hier; manche tanzen und singen, manche unterhalten sich und manche nehmen an verschiedenen Wettbewerben teil>

Linus: Los geht's!

<Siehe! Linus rennt auf einen Tisch mit vielen köstlichen Kuchen zu>

Saphira: Oje ... Linus wird es bestimmt wieder übertreiben ...

Zwerg: Es ist Zeit, den Gott des Bergbaus zu preisen! Bitte erhebt eure Humpen! Hip, hip, hurrah!

<Alle Zwerge trinken ihren Humpen aus. Linus hört auf zu essen und kratzt sich hinter seinem linken Ohr. Ein paar Sekunden sind vergangen. Linus fährt mit dem Essen fort>

Zwerg: Ich danke euch allen! Habt Spaß!

<Ein Zwerg mit einem schönen Hut ist gerade in den Fluss gefallen, der entlang des Landguts verläuft. Saphira rennt zu ihm ...>

Saphira: Are you ok?

\<The dwarf with the hat is laughing\>

Dwarf With a Hat: Yes, thank you; I'm fine!

\<Saphira is helping the dwarf get out of the river now\>

Linus: Saphira! Please help me!

\<Saphira is running to Linus\>

Saphira: What's the matter?

Linus: I'm unable to move!

\<Saphira is laughing\>

Saphira: You look like a ball!

Linus: This is not funny! How can I get back home now?

\<Saphira is grinning grimly\>

Linus: Saphira?!

Saphira: Bist du ok?

<Der Zwerg mit dem Hut lacht>

Zwerg mit einem Hut: Ja, danke; mir geht's gut!

<Saphira hilft nun dem Zwerg aus dem Fluss>

Linus: Saphira! Bitte hilf mir!

<Saphira rennt zu Linus>

Saphira: Was ist los?

Linus: Ich kann mich nicht bewegen!

<Saphira lacht>

Saphira: Du siehst aus wie ein Ball!

Linus: Das ist nicht lustig! Wie soll ich jetzt nach Hause kommen?

<Saphira grinst finster>

Linus: Saphira?!

<Saphira is casting a spell, and right now Linus is flying through the air>

Linus: Aaah!

Saphira: You should arrive home in a few minutes, Linus! Bye-bye!

<Saphira is laughing>

<Saphira wirkt einen Zauber und genau jetzt fliegt Linus durch die Luft>

Linus: Aaah!

Saphira: Du solltest in ein paar Minuten zu Hause sein, Linus! Tschüssi!

<Saphira lacht>

8 The Poisoned Holy Spring

<Saphira and Linus are having breakfast. Linus is eating a carrot>

Linus: Hm, this carrot tastes strange ...

<Behold! Linus is falling from his chair>

Saphira: Linus?! What's the matter? Are you not feeling well?

<Linus doesn't answer. It seems that he's fallen asleep>

Saphira: What should I do? We bought this carrot from farmer Trevor this morning. So, I'll go to him and ask him why he sold a poisoned carrot to us!

<Saphira has just arrived at farmer Trevor's farm>

Saphira: Trevor! Where are you?

Trevor: Ah, Saphira! I'm pleased that you visit me. What can I do for you?

8 Die vergiftete heilige Quelle

<Saphira und Linus frühstücken gerade. Linus isst eine Karotte>

Linus: Hm, diese Karotte schmeckt seltsam ...

<Siehe! Linus fällt von seinem Stuhl>

Saphira: Linus?! Was ist los? Fühlst du dich nicht gut?

<Linus antwortet nicht. Es scheint, dass er eingeschlafen ist>

Saphira: Was soll ich tun? Wir haben diese Karotte heute Morgen von Bauer Trevor gekauft. Also, ich werde zu ihm gehen und ihn fragen, warum er uns eine vergiftete Karotte verkauft hat!

<Saphira ist gerade auf Bauer Trevors Bauernhof angekommen>

Saphira: Trevor! Wo bist du?

Trevor: Ah, Saphira! Ich freue mich, dass du mich besuchst. Was kann ich für dich tun?

Saphira: Linus is ill! You've poisoned him with one of your carrots!

<Trevor is horrified>

Trevor: That's a lie! I wouldn't do anything like that! Somebody must have poisoned my carrots!

<Saphira notices a strange-looking liquid in a bucket>

Saphira: What's that for a liquid?

Trevor: That's water from the Holy Spring in the forest.

Saphira: That's it! Maybe somebody has poisoned the water!

Trevor: Let's go to the spring and find it out!

<A few minutes have passed. Now Saphira and Trevor are standing in front of the spring>

Saphira: Look! Over there are imps playing with different potions!

Saphira: Linus ist krank! Du hast ihn mit einer deiner Karotten vergiftet!

<Trevor ist entsetzt>

Trevor: Das ist eine Lüge! Ich würde so etwas nicht tun! Jemand muss meine Karotten vergiftet haben!

<Saphira bemerkt eine seltsame Flüssigkeit in einem Eimer>

Saphira: Was ist das für eine Flüssigkeit?

Trevor: Das ist Wasser von der heiligen Quelle im Wald.

Saphira: Das ist es! Vielleicht hat jemand das Wasser vergiftet!

Trevor: Lass uns zur Quelle gehen und es herausfinden!

<Ein paar Minuten sind vergangen. Nun stehen Saphira und Trevor vor der Quelle>

Saphira: Schau! Dort drüben sind Kobolde, die mit verschiedenen Tränken spielen!

Trevor: What should we do?

Saphira: I'll try to drive them away from the spring ... Hey, you imps!

<The imps have stopped playing and are looking to Saphira now>

Saphira: Please give me the potions! They are dangerous!

<The imps are laughing>

Saphira: Believe me! It's better for you to give me the potions!

<The imps are talking to each other. A few minutes have passed. One of the imps has just taken the potions, and now he's throwing them to Saphira>

Saphira: I think I can catch them!

<Saphira has caught all but one of the potions. The imps are laughing>

Trevor: Wow, pretty good! You only missed one potion.

Trevor: Was sollen wir tun?

Saphira: Ich werde versuchen, sie von der Quelle zu vertreiben ... Hey, ihr Kobolde!

<Die Kobolde haben aufgehört zu spielen und schauen nun zu Saphira>

Saphira: Bitte gebt mir die Tränke! Sie sind gefährlich!

<Die Kobolde lachen>

Saphira: Glaubt mir! Es ist besser für euch mir die Tränke zu geben!

<Die Kobolde sprechen miteinander. Ein paar Minuten sind vergangen. Einer der Kobolde hat gerade die Tränke genommen und wirft sie nun zu Saphira>

Saphira: Ich denke, ich kann sie fangen!

<Saphira hat alle bis auf einen Trank gefangen. Die Kobolde lachen>

Trevor: Wow, ziemlich gut! Du hast nur einen Trank verfehlt.

<Saphira has just put the potions on the ground and is casting a spell now. A loud bang can be heard, and the imps are running away>

Trevor: So, now that the imps are gone, the water should be fine again.

Saphira: No, it's still poisoned ...

Trevor: I've got an idea! I'll pray to the goddess who blessed this spring a long time ago.

Saphira: Ok.

<Trevor has prayed to the goddess, and the spring is shining in different colours now>

Trevor: She's blessed it again! Thank you!

Saphira: Fortunately, I always take a little bottle with me. I'll fill it up with the blessed water and try to heal Linus with it.

Trevor: Sounds good!

<Saphira hat gerade die Tränke auf den Boden gestellt und wirkt nun einen Zauber. Man kann einen lauten Knall hören und die Kobolde rennen davon>

Trevor: So, nun, da die Kobolde fort sind, sollte das Wasser wieder in Ordnung sein.

Saphira: Nein, es ist noch immer vergiftet ...

Trevor: Ich habe eine Idee! Ich werde zu der Göttin, die diese Quelle vor langer Zeit gesegnet hat, beten.

Saphira: Ok.

<Trevor hat zu der Göttin gebetet und die Quelle leuchtet nun in verschiedenen Farben>

Trevor: Sie hat sie erneut gesegnet! Danke!

Saphira: Glücklicherweise habe ich immer eine kleine Flasche bei mir. Ich werde sie mit dem gesegneten Wasser füllen und versuchen, Linus damit zu heilen.

Trevor: Hört sich gut an!

<Saphira is at home again>

Saphira: Linus, please drink this water.

<Linus doesn't open his mouth>

Saphira: I think it should work if I pour the water over him, too.

<Now Saphira is pouring the water over Linus>

Linus: Hey, why are you pouring water over me?

Saphira: Linus! You're fine! I'll tell you later ...

<Saphira ist wieder zu Hause>

Saphira: Linus, bitte trink dieses Wasser.

<Linus öffnet seinen Mund nicht>

Saphira: Ich denke, es sollte auch funktionieren, wenn ich das Wasser über ihn gieße.

<Jetzt gießt Saphira das Wasser über Linus>

Linus: Hey, warum gießt du Wasser über mich?

Saphira: Linus! Dir geht es gut! Ich werde es dir später sagen ...

9 Saphira and the Secret Book of Magic

<Linus is running to Saphira excitedly>

Linus: Saphira! I've just read something very interesting in an old book!

Saphira: I'm surprised that you read books!

Linus: It is said that the 'Vinegar Castle' has got a hidden entrance which leads to a room with a book called 'The Secret Book of Magic'!

Saphira: Ah, now that you mention it … I heard from that story some time ago ...

Linus: Let us go there and see if we can find the entrance and then the book!

Saphira: Hm … I think we should give it a try, ok!

<Linus is jumping up and down because he's happy>

Linus: Let's go!

9 Saphira und das geheime Buch der Magie

<Linus rennt gerade aufgeregt zu Saphira>

Linus: Saphira! Ich habe gerade etwas sehr Interessantes in einem alten Buch gelesen!

Saphira: Ich bin überrascht, dass du Bücher liest!

Linus: Man sagt, dass die „Essigburg" einen versteckten Eingang hat, der zu einem Raum mit einem Buch mit dem Titel „Das geheime Buch der Magie" führt!

Saphira: Ah, nun, da du es erwähnst … Ich habe vor geraumer Zeit von der Geschichte gehört ...

Linus: Lass uns dorthin gehen und schauen, ob wir den Eingang und dann das Buch finden!

Saphira: Hm … ich denke, wir sollten es versuchen, ok!

<Linus springt auf und ab, weil er glücklich ist>

Linus: Lass uns gehen!

<Saphira and Linus walked through the forest, met two wanderers on their way with whom they had a little talk, and had a rest at a charming inn. Now they are standing in front of the Vinegar Castle>

Linus: Wow! What a picturesque castle!

Saphira: Indeed ...

Linus: Hm … where could that hidden entrance be?

Saphira: Let me try to find it with a spell that I've recently learned.

<Saphira is casting a spell now>

Linus: And now?

Saphira: It works! I can see the entrance! It's under your paws!

Linus: Hey, that's cool – let's open it!

<Behold! The entrance is opening by itself>

<Saphira und Linus liefen durch den Wald, trafen auf ihrem Weg zwei Wanderer, mit denen sie einen kleinen Schwatz hielten und rasteten in einem reizenden Gasthof. Nun stehen sie vor der Essigburg>

Linus: Wow! Was für eine malerische Burg!

Saphira: In der Tat ...

Linus: Hm … wo könnte der versteckte Eingang sein?

Saphira: Lass mich ihn mit einem Zauber, den ich kürzlich gelernt habe, versuchen zu finden.

<Saphira wirkt nun einen Zauber>

Linus: Und nun?

Saphira: Es funktioniert! Ich kann den Eingang sehen! Er befindet sich unter deinen Pfoten!

Linus: Hey, Das ist cool – lass uns ihn öffnen!

<Siehe! Der Eingang öffnet sich von alleine>

Saphira: We must be careful! We don't know what's down there!

Linus: You're right!

<Linus is brandishing his warhammer now. A few minutes have passed. Now Saphira and Linus are walking along a long corridor>

Linus: Ah! Over there are armed skeletons!

Saphira: I'll blow them away!

<Saphira has cast a spell. A big fireball has destroyed the skeletons>

Linus: Nice!

<Saphira is smiling>

Saphira: I … I can feel that the book is near ...

Linus: Wow! That's female intuition!

Saphira: Here it is!

Saphira: Wir müssen vorsichtig sein! Wir wissen nicht, was dort unten ist!

Linus: Du hast recht!

<Linus schwingt nun seinen Kriegshammer. Ein paar Minuten sind vergangen. Nun gehen Saphira und Linus einen langen Korridor entlang>

Linus: Ah! Dort drüben sind bewaffnete Skelette!

Saphira: Ich werde sie wegpusten!

<Saphira hat einen Zauber gewirkt. Ein großer Feuerball hat die Skelette zerstört>

Linus: Schön!

<Saphira lächelt>

Saphira: Ich … ich kann fühlen, dass das Buch nahe ist …

Linus: Wow! Das ist weibliche Intuition!

Saphira: Hier ist es!

<Behold! Saphira is holding an old book in her hands>

Linus: I can't believe it! The Secret Book of Magic really exists! Let's take it and return home.

Saphira: Yes, let's do that.

<Suddenly, the book has disappeared>

Linus: Where is the book?!

Saphira: I don't know — it's gone!

Voice: You must not take this book with you! It has to be kept in this castle! Go away from here and never come back!

Linus: Who are you?

Voice: Once I used to be a wizard and wrote this book when I was young … Please, leave me now!

Linus: No! We've come here to take it to our house so that Saphira can study it!

<Siehe! Saphira hält ein altes Buch in ihren Händen>

Linus: Ich kann es nicht glauben! Das geheime Buch der Magie existiert wirklich! Lass es uns nehmen und nach Hause zurückkehren.

Saphira: Ja, lass uns das tun.

<Plötzlich ist das Buch verschwunden>

Linus: Wo ist das Buch?!

Saphira: Ich weiß es nicht – es ist fort!

Stimme: Ihr dürft das Buch nicht mitnehmen! Es muss in dieser Burg aufbewahrt werden! Geht weg von hier und kehrt nie zurück!

Linus: Wer bist du?

Stimme: Einst war ich Zauberer und schrieb dieses Buch, als ich jung war … Bitte, verlasst mich nun!

Linus: Nein! Wir sind hierher gekommen, um das Buch mit nach Hause zu nehmen, sodass Saphira es dort studieren kann!

Voice: Saphira? If you are a wizard, I'm willing to give you permission to study it here in my former study.

Saphira: Thank you … But it's a long way from home to this castle …

Voice: No problem! Are you able to use a teleport spell?

Saphira: Yes … Ah, I got it! You mean I could teleport myself to this place whenever I'd like to read the book, right?

Voice: Yes.

Linus: Well, if Saphira is fine with it, I'm too.

Saphira: Ok, I'll do so. Thank you for your permission.

Linus: Well, let's go back home …

Stimme: Saphira? Wenn du eine Zauberin bist, bin ich willens, dir die Erlaubnis zu geben, das Buch hier in meinem ehemaligen Studierzimmer zu studieren.

Saphira: Danke … Aber es ist ein langer Weg von zu Hause bis zu dieser Burg ...

Stimme: Kein Problem! Bist du fähig, einen Teleportzauber zu wirken?

Saphira: Ja … Ah, ich habe verstanden! Du meinst, dass ich mich an diesen Ort teleportieren könnte, wann immer ich das Buch lesen möchte, richtig?

Stimme: Ja.

Linus: Nun, wenn Saphira damit einverstanden ist, bin ich es auch.

Saphira: Ok, das werde ich machen. Danke für deine Erlaubnis.

Linus: Nun, lass uns nach Hause gehen ...

10 A Shadow in the Temple

<Saphira and Linus are in the temple to visit their friend Tirzah>

Tirzah: I'm so happy that you're here!

Linus: Please hug and kiss me because I'm a cute hamster!

<Tirzah is laughing>

Tirzah: Of course!

Saphira: You look as beautiful as ever, Tirzah! You seem to enjoy the work in the temple.

Tirzah: Yes, I love to help other people and –

Linus: Please caress my fleecy belly that tickles so nicely!

<Tirzah is laughing. Saphira grabs Linus and puts him on her right shoulder>

Saphira: That's enough! Stay here now!

10 Ein Schatten im Tempel

<Saphira und Linus sind im Tempel, um ihre Freundin Tirzah zu besuchen>

Tirzah: Ich bin so glücklich, dass ihr hier seid!

Linus: Bitte knuddle mich, weil ich ein süßer Hamster bin!

<Tirzah lacht>

Tirzah: Natürlich!

Saphira: Du siehst so hübsch wie immer aus, Tirzah! Du scheinst die Arbeit im Tempel zu genießen.

Tirzah: Ja, ich liebe es, anderen Menschen zu helfen –

Linus: Bitte streichle meinen flauschigen Bauch, das kitzelt so schön!

<Tirzah lacht. Saphira schnappt Linus und setzt ihn auf ihre rechte Schulter>

Saphira: Das reicht! Bleib jetzt hier!

Linus: Spoilsport!

<Now a priestess is coming to Tirzah in a hurry>

Priestess: Tirzah! There is something wrong with the little chapel ...

Tirzah: All right, I'll come with you! Saphira and Linus, please follow me!

<The priestess, Tirzah, Saphira, and Linus are standing in the chapel>

Saphira: It's very dark in here ... even though it's noon and the sun is shining!

Tirzah: Yes, that's strange ... This place is normally peaceful and beautiful.

<The priestess is laughing, and now her eyes are turning red>

Priestess: Now I'll kill you!

Linus: No way! You are a demon – or are you Saphira's grandmother?

Linus: Spielverderberin!

<Nun kommt eine Priesterin eilig zu Tirzah>

Priesterin: Tirzah! Irgendetwas stimmt nicht mit der kleinen Kapelle ...

Tirzah: Alles klar, ich komme mit dir! Saphira und Linus, bitte folgt mir!

<Die Priesterin, Tirzah, Saphira und Linus stehen in der Kapelle>

Saphira: Es ist sehr dunkel hier drinnen ... obwohl es Mittag ist und die Sonne scheint!

Tirzah: Ja, das ist seltsam … Dieser Ort ist normalerweise friedvoll und schön.

<Die Priesterin lacht und nun werden ihre Augen rot>

Priesterin: Jetzt werde ich euch töten!

Linus: Keine Chance! Du bist eine Dämonin – oder Saphiras Großmutter?

Saphira: Stop that, Linus!

Tirzah: I can't fight! I'm a priestess, not a warrior or anything like that!

<Linus is laughing>

Linus: Leave it to me! Oh … I've forgotten my warhammer ...

<Saphira is rolling her eyes>

Saphira: We must try to drive out the evil spirit from her body!

Tirzah: Yes … Please try to stop her! I'm back in a few minutes!

Saphira: Ok!

Linus: What should we do, Saphira?

<Behold! The priestess is attacking Saphira with a knife>

Saphira: Ah!

Saphira: Hör auf damit, Linus!

Tirzah: Ich kann nicht kämpfen! Ich bin Priesterin und keine Kriegerin oder so etwas in der Art!

<Linus lacht>

Linus: Überlasse das mir! Oh … ich habe meinen Kriegshammer vergessen …

<Saphira verdreht die Augen>

Saphira: Wir müssen versuchen, den bösen Geist aus ihrem Körper zu treiben!

Tirzah: Ja … Bitte versucht sie aufzuhalten! Ich bin in ein paar Minuten zurück!

Saphira: Ok!

Linus: Was sollen wir tun, Saphira?

<Siehe! Die Priesterin attackiert Saphira mit einem Messer>

Saphira: Ah!

<Linus has jumped onto the priestess, and now he's biting and scratching her wherever he can>

Saphira: I … I must cast a spell to protect me ...

<Now Tirzah is coming back with two other priestesses>

Tirzah: Saphira! We must help her immediately!

Two Priestesses: Yes!

<Tirzah and the two priestesses are chanting an old verse>

Priest: Ah ...

<The priestess has collapsed, and now a strange mist is coming out of her>

Tirzah: That's the evil spirit!

<Saphira is casting a spell>

<Linus ist auf die Priesterin gesprungen und beißt und kratzt sie nun, wo immer er kann>

Saphira: Ich … ich muss versuchen, einen Zauber zu wirken, um mich zu schützen ...

<Jetzt kommt Tirzah zusammen mit zwei anderen Priesterinnen>

Tirzah: Saphira! Wir müssen ihr sofort helfen!

Zwei Priesterinnen: Ja!

<Tirzah und die beiden Priesterinnen sprechen einen alten Vers>

Priesterin: Ah ...

<Die Priesterin ist zusammengebrochen und jetzt kommt ein seltsamer Nebel aus ihr heraus>

Tirzah: Das ist der böse Geist!

<Saphira wirkt einen Zauber>

Saphira: Back to hell!

<A dazzling white light has appeared that is sucking in the strange mist now. A few minutes have passed. The white light and the strange mist have disappeared>

Linus: You did it!

Priestess: I'm so tired ...

Tirzah: Don't worry, we'll soon have you back on your feet again.

Saphira: Zurück in die Hölle!

<Ein blendend weißes Licht ist erschienen, das nun den seltsamen Nebel einsaugt. Ein paar Minuten sind vergangen. Das weiße Licht und der seltsame Nebel sind verschwunden>

Linus: Ihr habt's geschafft!

Priesterin: Ich bin so müde ...

Tirzah: Keine Sorge, wir werden dich bald wieder auf die Beine bringen.

11 A Birthday Present for Linus

<It's a sunny day in June. The sky is free of clouds, and a gentle breeze is blowing. Saphira is working in her room while thinking about a birthday present for Linus>

Saphira: Linus loves sweet things, so I think I should go to a cake shop and buy a delicious gateau!

<Saphira is smiling>

Saphira: ONE gateau? No, TWO gateaux! I know that he is a little greedy-guts ...

<Saphira is laughing>

Saphira: Yes, that's it! Two gateaux with his name written on them!

<Saphira has come to the local cake shop>

Confectioner: Can I help you?

Saphira: I'd like to order two gateaux with the name 'Linus' written on them.

11 Ein Geburtstagsgeschenk für Linus

<Es ist ein sonniger Tag im Juni. Der Himmel ist frei von Wolken und es weht eine sanfte Brise. Saphira arbeitet gerade in ihrem Zimmer, während sie über ein Geburtstagsgeschenk für Linus nachdenkt>

Saphira: Linus liebt süße Dinge, also denke ich, dass ich in eine Konditorei gehen und eine köstliche Torte kaufen sollte!

<Saphira lächelt>

Saphira: EINE Torte? Nein, ZWEI Torten! Ich weiß, dass er ein kleiner Nimmersatt ist ...

<Saphira lacht>

Saphira: Ja, das ist es! Zwei Torten, auf denen sein Name geschrieben steht!

<Saphira ist zur örtlichen Konditorei gekommen>

Konditor: Du wünschst?

Saphira: Ich möchte zwei Torten, auf denen „Linus" geschrieben steht, kaufen.

Confectioner: Very well, you can collect them tomorrow in the afternoon.

Saphira: That's great! Thank you!

<Saphira is back home>

Linus: Hey, where have you been? Normally, you study in your room at this time of day.

Saphira: Yes, but I've just had to do something very important ...

Linus: Something VERY important?

<Linus is staring at Saphira's hair now>

Linus: Well, your haircut looks like your old one ...

Saphira: Hey, my haircut is fine! I like it!

<Linus is laughing>

Konditor: Sehr gerne, du kannst sie morgen am Nachmittag abholen.

Saphira: Das ist großartig! Danke!

<Saphira ist zurück zu Hause>

Linus: Hey, wo bist du gewesen? Normalerweise studierst du zu dieser Tageszeit in deinem Zimmer.

Saphira: Ja, aber ich habe gerade etwas sehr Wichtiges zu erledigen gehabt ...

Linus: Etwas SEHR Wichtiges?

<Linus starrt nun auf Saphiras Haar>

Linus: Also, dein Haarschnitt sieht wie der alte aus ...

Saphira: Hey, mein Haarschnitt ist in Ordnung! Ich mag ihn!

<Linus lacht>

Linus: Ah, now I've got it! Tomorrow is my birthday! You probably have prepared a surprise for me ...

Saphira: Who knows?

<It's Linus' birthday>

Linus: I'm one year older now, but I'm still a young buck!

<Now Linus is laughing while doing some exercises>

Saphira: Linus! Two 'guests' are waiting here for you! Don't let them wait!

Linus: Eh? Guests?! Hopefully, not my cousins Brutus and Quintus … Brutus always stinks like my old, worn-out socks … and Quintus is a coward ... Yes, I'm coming!

Saphira: Happy birthday, dear Linus! Here are the two 'guests'!

<Behold! Saphira is revealing the table with a spell>

Linus: Ah, nun hab ich es! Morgen ist mein Geburtstag! Du hast wahrscheinlich eine Überraschung für mich vorbereitet ...

Saphira: Wer weiß?

<Es ist Linus' Geburtstag>

Linus: Ich bin nun ein Jahr älter, aber ich bin immer noch ein Jungspund!

<Nun lacht Linus, während er ein paar Fitnessübungen macht>

Saphira: Linus! Zwei „Gäste" warten hier auf dich! Lass sie nicht warten!

Linus: Äh? Gäste?! Hoffentlich nicht meine Cousins Brutus und Quintus … Brutus stinkt immer wie meine alten, abgenutzten Socken … und Quintus ist ein Feigling ... Ja, ich komme!

Saphira: Alles Gute zum Geburtstag, lieber Linus! Hier sind die beiden „Gäste"!

<Siehe! Saphira lässt den Tisch mit einem Zauber sichtbar werden>

Linus: Wow! Two marvellous gateaux! Thank you so much, Saphira! Let's eat them!

<Linus has jumped onto one of the gateaux>

Linus: Wow! Zwei wundervolle Torten! Ich danke dir so sehr, Saphira! Lass sie uns essen!

<Linus ist auf eine der beiden Torten gesprungen>

12 Saphira Is Missing

\<It's late at night, and Linus is waking up ...\>

Linus: Oh dear, I can't sleep for some reason ... I think I should get myself a book from our little library ...

\<Linus is on the way to the library\>

Linus: The door to Saphira's bedroom is open ... That's strange ... Saphira, are you all right?

\<Nobody is answering. Now Linus is entering Saphira's bedroom\>

Linus: She's gone! Saphira? Where are you? Saphira!

\<Linus notices a piece of fur on the floor\>

Linus: I know this kind of fur! It's from a werewolf! Hm, what should I do? … Yes! First, I'll get my warhammer, and then I'll try to find the werewolf and Saphira! I'll smack a werewolf's butt tonight, yeah!

\<Now Linus is searching around the house\>

12 Saphira wird vermisst

<Es ist spät in der Nacht und Linus wacht gerade auf ...>

Linus: Oje, aus irgendeinem Grund kann ich nicht schlafen … Ich denke, ich sollte mir ein Buch aus unserer kleinen Bibliothek holen ...

<Linus ist auf dem Weg zur Bibliothek>

Linus: Die Tür zu Saphiras Schlafzimmer steht offen … Das ist komisch ... Saphira, bist du in Ordnung?

<Niemand antwortet. Nun betritt Linus Saphiras Schlafzimmer>

Linus: Sie ist fort! Saphira? Wo bist du? Saphira!

<Linus bemerkt ein Stück Fell auf dem Boden>

Linus: Ich kenne diese Art von Fell! Es ist von einem Werwolf! Hm, was soll ich tun? … Ja! Zuerst werde ich meinen Kriegshammer holen und dann werde ich versuchen, den Werwolf und Saphira zu finden! Ich werde heute Nacht den Hintern eines Werwolfs versohlen, yeah!

<Nun sucht Linus um das Haus herum>

Linus: Hm, no trace of the werewolf or Saphira ...

<Behold! A little bat is flying around Linus>

Linus: Hey, what are you doing?!

<The little bat is laughing>

Bat: Are you searching for Saphira?

Linus: I don't know if I can trust you ... Maybe you want to blackmail me ...

Bat: Why would I blackmail you?

Linus: Because you may know where Saphira is ...

Bat: Ah, you ARE searching for Saphira!

Linus: Damn! Yes I am! Don't try to fool me, or this lovely warhammer will smash your damn skull!

<The bat is laughing>

Linus: Hm, keine Spur von dem Werwolf oder Saphira ...

<Siehe! Eine kleine Fledermaus fliegt um Linus herum>

Linus: Hey, was tust du?!

<Die kleine Fledermaus lacht>

Fledermaus: Suchst du Saphira?

Linus: Ich weiß nicht, ob ich dir trauen kann … Vielleicht willst du mich erpressen ...

Fledermaus: Warum sollte ich dich erpressen?

Linus: Weil du vielleicht weißt, wo Saphira ist ...

Fledermaus: Ah, du suchst also nach Saphira!

Linus: Verdammt! Ja, das tue ich! Versuche nicht, mich zum Narren zu halten, sonst wird dieser liebliche Kriegshammer deinen verdammten Schädel zerschmettern!

<Die Fledermaus lacht>

Bat: You are so funny! Trust me, I just want to help you find Saphira!

Linus: Ok, then tell me where Saphira is!

Bat: A stupid werewolf has brought her to my cave ...

Linus: To your cave? Did you ask the werewolf to kidnap her?!

Bat: No, I didn't. Please follow me!

Linus: Ok.

<The bat is leading Linus to its cave now>

Bat: Here we are! Isn't it a beautiful cave?

Linus: Hm, not bad ... But don't you have any cuddly toys?

Bat: Cuddly toys?! Are you mad?!

Linus: I don't know what you mean. I love cuddly toys! I –

Fledermaus: Du bist so witzig! Vertraue mir, ich will dir nur helfen, Saphira zu finden!

Linus: Ok, dann sag mir, wo Saphira ist!

Fledermaus: Ein dummer Werwolf hat sie in meine Höhle gebracht ...

Linus: In deine Höhle? Hast du den Werwolf darum gebeten, Saphira zu entführen?!

Fledermaus: Nein. Bitte folge mir!

Linus: Ok.

<Die Fledermaus führt nun Linus zu ihrer Höhle>

Fledermaus: Hier sind wir! Ist das nicht eine schöne Höhle?

Linus: Hm, nicht schlecht … Aber hast du gar keine Knuddeltiere?

Fledermaus: Knuddeltiere?! Bist du verrückt?!

Linus: Ich weiß nicht, was du meinst. Ich liebe Knuddeltiere! Ich –

Bat: Shut up! If you walk a bit deeper into the cave, you'll find Saphira ...

<Linus has been walking for a few minutes now>

Linus: Ah, over there she is! Saphira!

Saphira: I'm so happy to see you, Linus! How did you find me?

Linus: A cute, little bat helped me find you ...

Saphira: That's nice of it!

<Suddenly, the werewolf has appeared>

Werewolf: You must not take her away from me!

Linus: You see this beautifully crafted warhammer? It's just told me that it would like to smack your butt!

<Behold! The werewolf is getting angry>

Werewolf: And I want to eat you!

Fledermaus: Halt die Klappe! Wenn du ein bisschen tiefer in die Höhle hineingehst, dann wirst du Saphira finden ...

<Linus ist nun schon ein paar Minuten lang gelaufen>

Linus: Ah, dort drüben ist sie! Saphira!

Saphira: Ich bin so glücklich dich zu sehen, Linus! Wie hast du mich gefunden?

Linus: Eine süße, kleine Fledermaus hat mir geholfen, dich zu finden ...

Saphira: Das ist lieb von ihr!

<Plötzlich ist der Werwolf erschienen>

Werwolf: Du darfst sie mir nicht wegnehmen!

Linus: Siehst du diesen schön gefertigten Kriegshammer? Er hat mir gerade gesagt, dass er gerne deinen Hinter versohlen möchte!

<Siehe! Der Werwolf wird zornig>

Werwolf: Und ich will dich fressen!

<Now the werewolf is running towards Linus, while Linus is yawning. The werewolf is just a few steps away from Linus, and now Linus is hitting the werewolf with his warhammer over and over again>

Werewolf: Please stop that!

<The werewolf is crying>

Linus: Eh, that sounds like the voice of the little bat!

<Behold! The little bat is coming out of the werewolf's head>

Saphira: That's a kind of machine that looks like a werewolf!

Linus: I can't believe it!

Bat: Please forgive me! I'm so interested in magic, alchemy, and building different kinds of machines. I thought that if I kidnapped Saphira, she would teach me more things.

<Nun rennt der Werwolf auf Linus zu, während Linus gähnt. Der Werwolf ist nur ein paar Schritte von Linus entfernt, und nun schlägt Linus immer und immer wieder den Werwolf mit seinem Kriegshammer>

Werwolf: Bitte höre damit auf!

<Der Werwolf weint>

Linus: Äh, das hört sich wie die Stimme der kleinen Fledermaus an!

<Siehe! Die Fledermaus kommt aus dem Kopf des Werwolfs>

Saphira: Das ist eine Art Maschine, die wie ein Werwolf aussieht!

Linus: Ich kann es nicht glauben!

Fledermaus: Bitte vergebt mir! Ich interessiere mich so für Magie, Alchemie und für das Bauen verschiedener Maschinen. Ich dachte, wenn ich Saphira entführte, würde sie mir weitere Dinge beibringen.

Saphira: Why didn't you just ask me to teach you?

Bat: I thought that you might be afraid of me and wouldn't teach me without paying you for that.

Saphira: I wouldn't have taken money for teaching you. Anyway, everything is fine. If you like, I'll come here twice a week and teach you.

<The bat's eyes are shining now>

Bat: Thank you so much!

Saphira: Warum hast du mich nicht einfach gebeten, dich zu unterrichten?

Fledermaus: Ich dachte, du könntest dich vor mir fürchten und würdest mich ohne dich dafür zu entlohnen nicht unterrichten.

Saphira: Ich hätte kein Geld dafür genommen, dich zu unterrichten. Wie dem auch sei, alles ist in Ordnung. Wenn du möchtest, werde ich immer zweimal die Woche herkommen und dich unterrichten.

<Die Augen der Fledermaus strahlen nun>

Fledermaus: Ich danke dir so sehr!

13 The Treasure of the Old Man Is ...

Linus: It's so relaxing sitting in the hammock and looking to the sky ... It's so peaceful and ... Oh, my left ear is itching!

<Linus is scratching himself now>

Linus: Aaah, that's pleasant!

<Now Saphira is coming into the garden>

Saphira: You are so lazy, Linus!

Linus: Come on, I've worked enough for today ...

<Saphira is laughing>

Saphira: You mean eating four portions of noodles, three carrots, and two big pieces of your favourite cake?

Linus: Well ...

<An old man is shouting>

13 Der Schatz des alten Mannes ist ...

Linus: Es ist so entspannend, in der Hängematte zu liegen und in den Himmel zu schauen ... Es ist so friedlich und … Oh, mein linkes Ohr juckt!

<Linus kratzt sich nun>

Linus: Aaah, das ist angenehm!

<Jetzt kommt Saphira in den Garten>

Saphira: Du bist so faul, Linus!

Linus: Komm schon, ich habe genug für heute gearbeitet ...

<Saphira lacht>

Saphira: Du meinst, vier Portionen Nudeln, drei Karotten und zwei große Stücke deines Lieblingskuchens essen?

Linus: Also ...

<Ein alter Mann schreit>

Old Man: Where's my beloved treasure? I can't find it anywhere! Maybe this fat hamster has stolen it ...

Linus: A fat hamster? Who could he mean?

<Saphira is rolling her eyes>

Saphira: Wait here for a moment, please. I'll go to the old man and ask him what his problem is ...

Old Man: Ah, you are Saphira, right? You are a wizard ... or a barmaid?

Saphira: Yes, I'm a wizard!

Old Man: My beloved treasure is gone! Please, help me find it!

Saphira: Sure – but what is your treasure?

Old Man: I can't remember ... I'm so excited that it's gone, that I just can't remember ...

Saphira: Oh dear ...

Alter Mann: Wo ist mein geliebter Schatz? Ich kann ihn nirgendwo finden! Vielleicht hat dieser fette Hamster ihn gestohlen ...

Linus: Ein fetter Hamster? Wen könnte er meinen?

<Saphira verdreht die Augen>

Saphira: Bitte warte hier einen Moment. Ich gehe zum alten Mann und frage ihn, was sein Problem ist ...

Alter Mann: Ah, du bist Saphira, richtig? Du bist eine Zauberin ... oder eine Schankmaid?

Saphira: Ja, ich bin eine Zauberin!

Alter Mann: Mein geliebter Schatz ist fort! Bitte hilf mir, ihn zu finden!

Saphira: Sicher – aber was ist dein Schatz?

Alter Mann: Ich kann mich nicht erinnern ... Ich bin so aufgeregt darüber, dass er fort ist, dass ich mich einfach nicht erinnern kann ...

Saphira: Oje ...

<Now Linus is coming>

Old Man: You! You stinky hamster! You must have stolen my treasure!

<The old man has just grabbed Linus and is shaking him now>

Linus: S-stop that! I'm getting dizzy!

Saphira: Stop that, please!

Old Man: All right! No, you don't have my treasure. It should have fallen out of your pockets or so … Ah, or you've hidden it somewhere!

Linus: No! Don't touch me again! Believe me! I haven't stolen your treasure!

Old Man: All right, I believe you! Sorry, my hairy little friend.

Saphira: Over there! Something is lying under the tree!

<Nun kommt Linus>

Alter Mann: Du! Du stinkender Hamster! Du musst meinen Schatz gestohlen haben!

<Der alte Mann hat Linus geschnappt und schüttelt ihn nun>

Linus: H-hör auf damit! Mir wird schwindelig!

Saphira: Hör bitte damit auf!

Alter Mann: In Ordnung! Nein, du hast meinen Schatz nicht. Er hätte aus deinen Taschen fallen müssen oder so … Ah, oder du hast ihn irgendwo versteckt!

Linus: Nein! Fass mich nicht noch einmal an! Glaube mir! Ich habe deinen Schatz nicht gestohlen!

Alter Mann: In Ordnung, ich glaube dir! Entschuldigung, mein haariger, kleiner Freund.

Saphira: Dort drüben! Unter dem Baum liegt etwas!

<The old man is running to the tree now>

Old Man: Aaah!

Linus: What's happened?!

Old Man: My treasure!

<Behold! The old man is holding an old back-scratcher in the air>

Saphira: That's your treasure?!

Old Man: My beloved back-scratcher! You know what, Linus? Let's make up! I'll even scratch your back with my wonderful back-scratcher!

Linus: Noo!

<Linus is running away>

<Der alte Mann rennt nun zum Baum>

Alter Mann: Aaah!

Linus: Was ist geschehen?!

Alter Mann: Mein Schatz!

<Siehe! Der alte Mann hält einen alten Rückenkratzer in die Luft>

Saphira: Das ist dein Schatz?!

Alter Mann: Mein geliebter Rückenkratzer! Weißt du was, Linus? Lass uns versöhnen! Ich werde sogar deinen Rücken mit meinem wundervollen Rückenkratzer kratzen!

Linus: Neeein!

<Linus rennt davon>

14 Saphira Wants to Sing!

<It's a rainy and cold day in December. Saphira and Linus are sitting by the fireplace>

Saphira: I often think of taking singing lessons lately. What do you think about this?

<Linus is surprised>

Linus: Oh, well … you would be a great singer for sure ...

<Linus is grinning>

Saphira: Hey, why are you grinning? Perhaps I could even earn some money with singing ...

<Linus is laughing>

Linus: Sure, if you sang for orcs and trolls!

<Saphira is getting angry now. Linus has jumped onto Saphira's right shoulder>

14 Saphira will singen!

<Es ist ein verregneter und kalter Tag im Dezember. Saphira und Linus sitzen gerade vor dem Kamin>

Saphira: In letzter Zeit denke ich oft daran, Gesangsunterricht zu nehmen. Was hältst du davon?

<Linus ist überrascht>

Linus: Oh, also … du wärst bestimmt eine großartige Sängerin ...

<Linus grinst>

Saphira: Hey, warum grinst du? Vielleicht könnte ich mit dem Singen sogar Geld verdienen ...

<Linus lacht>

Linus: Sicher, wenn du für Orks und Trolle sängest!

<Saphira wird nun zornig. Linus ist auf Saphiras rechte Schulter gesprungen>

Linus: Hey, I've got an idea!

Saphira: Yes?

Linus: Oh yes, I'm pretty sure that you'll like it! I will teach you how to sing!

<Saphira is rolling her eyes>

Saphira: Yes … that's a wonderful idea …

Linus: I'm serious about this. Come on, Saphira! Let's begin right now!

<Now Linus is telling Saphira different things about how to sing correctly. He even knows a lot about music theory>

Saphira: I never would have thought that you'd know that much about music!

<Linus is smiling with his chest swelled with pride>

Linus: My uncle Titus is a very good musician. He often visited my family and taught me – it was always fun ...

Linus: Hey, ich habe eine Idee!

Saphira: Ja?

Linus: Oh ja, ich bin mir ziemlich sicher, dass du sie mögen wirst! ICH werde dir beibringen, zu singen!

<Saphira verdreht die Augen>

Saphira: Ja … das ist eine wundervolle Idee …

Linus: Es ist mir ernst! Komm schon, Saphira! Lass uns gleich damit beginnen!

<Jetzt erzählt Linus Saphira verschiedene Dinge darüber, wie man richtig singt. Er weiß sogar sehr viel über Musiktheorie>

Saphira: Ich hätte nie gedacht, dass du so viel über Musik wüsstest!

<Linus lächelt mit Stolz geschwellter Brust>

Linus: Mein Onkel Titus ist ein sehr guter Musiker. Er hat meine Familie häufig besucht und mich unterrichtet – es hat immer Spaß gemacht …

Saphira: I see – I'd like to try to sing a song!

Linus: Sure, here you are! Lyrics that my uncle wrote.

Saphira: Let me see ...

<Saphira is looking at the lyrics now>

Saphira: I love hamsters! Yes, I do! Nothing is more fleecy, nothing is more cuddly – it's just hamsters! Hurray!

Linus: YEAH!

Saphira: Eh … Well … not bad … I guess ...

Linus: It's genius! Sing it!

<Saphira is blushing>

Saphira: I love hamsters! Yes, I do! Nothing is more fleecy, nothing is more cuddly – it's just hamsters! Hurray!

Saphira: Verstehe – ich möchte versuchen, ein Lied zu singen!

Linus: Sicher, hier! Ein Liedtext, den mein Onkel geschrieben hat.

Saphira: Lass mich mal sehen ...

<Saphira sieht sich nun den Liedtext an>

Saphira: Ich liebe Hamster! Ja, das tue ich! Nichts ist flauschiger, nichts ist knuddeliger – einfach Hamster! Juhu!

Linus: JAWOLL!

Saphira: Äh … Nun … nicht schlecht … schätze ich ...

Linus: Es ist genial! Sing es!

<Saphira errötet>

Saphira: Ich liebe Hamster! Ja, das tue ich! Nichts ist flauschiger, nichts ist knuddeliger – einfach Hamster! Juhu!

<Now a tear is running down Linus' face>

Linus: Wonderful!

<Linus is applauding>

<Nun läuft eine Träne Linus' Gesicht hinunter>

Linus: Wundervoll!

<Linus applaudiert>

15 Arguing Wizards ...

\<Saphira is practising some spells ...\>

Saphira: That's great! Now I'll conjure a little blizzard!

\<A blizzard has appeared\>

Saphira: Oh no, I can't control it! Watch out! This blizzard is out of control!

\<Behold! The blizzard is moving towards a girl, who is walking along the meadow\>

Girl: Aaah!

\<The blizzard has just frozen the girl\>

Saphira: I'm so sorry! I'll help you!

\<The blizzard has disappeared, and now Saphira is casting a spell. A light red ray has just hit the frozen girl\>

15 Streitende Zauberinnen ...

\<Saphira übt gerade ein paar Zauber ...\>

Saphira: Das ist großartig! Nun werde ich einen kleinen Blizzard beschwören!

\<Ein Blizzard ist erschienen\>

Saphira: Oh nein, ich kann ihn nicht kontrollieren! Passt auf! Dieser Blizzard ist außer Kontrolle!

\<Siehe! Der Blizzard bewegt sich auf ein Mädchen zu, das die Wiese entlang läuft\>

Mädchen: Aaah!

\<Der Blizzard hat soeben das Mädchen eingefroren\>

Saphira: Es tut mir so leid! Ich werde dir helfen!

\<Der Blizzard ist verschwunden und nun wirkt Saphira einen Zauber. Ein hellroter Strahl hat soeben das eingefrorene Mädchen getroffen\>

Saphira: I hope it works ...

<A few seconds have passed. The girl isn't frozen anymore and is able to move again>

Girl: Hey, what the hell are you doing?!

Saphira: I'm so sorry! I was practising some spells, then I lost control of the blizzard ... Well, you know the rest of the story ...

Girl: Ha, you are a loser! I'm Evelyn McLee and a real wizard! I could beat you in a fight without any effort!

<Saphira is getting angry now>

Saphira: Really? Alright, let's have a little fight! Each of us summons an armed skeleton, and then we'll let them fight against each other. The one whose skeleton has defeated the other skeleton is the winner, ok?

Saphira: Ich hoffe, es funktioniert ...

<Ein paar Sekunden sind vergangen. Das Mädchen ist nicht länger eingefroren und kann sich wieder bewegen>

Mädchen: Hey, was zur Hölle treibst du?!

Saphira: Es tut mir so leid! Ich war dabei, Zauber zu üben, dann verlor ich die Kontrolle über den Blizzard ... Nun, den Rest der Geschichte kennst du ja ...

Mädchen: Ha, du bist eine Niete! Ich bin Evelyn McLee und eine WAHRE Zauberin! Ich könnte dich in einem Kampf ohne jegliche Anstrengung besiegen!

<Saphira wird nun zornig>

Saphira: Wirklich? Alles klar, lass uns einen kleinen Kampf austragen! Jeder von uns beschwört ein bewaffnetes Skelett und dann werden wir sie gegeneinander antreten lassen. Diejenige, deren Skelett das andere besiegt hat, ist die Siegerin, ok?

<Evelyn is laughing>

Evelyn: Sure, let's summon a simple skeleton. I'm really not surprised that you aren't able to summon anything better!

<Suddenly, Linus has come to them>

Linus: Hey, I saw you both arguing from the terrace a few minutes ago … You seem to be about to fight a duel ...

Saphira: Of course!

<Linus is smiling>

Linus: Well, let me be the referee!

Evelyn: Aaaaah!

<Behold! Evelyn is caressing Linus>

Evelyn: You are so cute!

<Evelyn lacht>

Evelyn: Sicher, lass uns ein einfaches Skelett beschwören. Ich bin wirklich nicht überrascht darüber, dass du nicht etwas Besseres beschwören kannst!

<Plötzlich ist Linus zu ihnen gekommen>

Linus: Hey, ich habe euch beide vor ein paar Minuten von der Terrasse aus streiten sehen … Ihr scheint im Begriff zu sein, euch zu duellieren ...

Saphira: Natürlich!

<Linus lächelt>

Linus: Nun, lasst mich der Schiedsrichter sein!

Evelyn: Aaaaah!

<Siehe! Evelyn streichelt Linus>

Evelyn: Du bist so süß!

<Linus is laughing>

Linus: I'm very ticklish on my belly!

Saphira: Stop that at once!

Evelyn: Oh, I almost forgot our fight ... Ok, let's summon our skeletons!

<Now Saphira and Evelyn are casting a spell>

Linus: Good luck to both of you!

Saphira: Both?! You betrayer!

<Both skeletons are standing facing each other>

Evelyn: Attack the little worm!

<Evelyn's skeleton is hitting Saphira's skeleton with a big axe over and over again>

Linus: Damn! Your skeleton is very powerful!

Evelyn: Thanks, cuddly hamster! But her skeleton is pretty weak ...

<Linus lacht>

Linus: Ich bin sehr kitzlig am Bauch!

Saphira: Hör sofort damit auf!

Evelyn: Oh, ich hätte beinahe unseren Kampf vergessen ... Ok, lass uns unsere Skelette beschwören!

<Nun wirken Saphira und Evelyn einen Zauber>

Linus: Viel Glück euch beiden!

Saphira: Beiden?! Du Verräter!

<Beide Skelette stehen sich gegenüber>

Evelyn: Greife den kleinen Wurm an!

<Evelyns Skelett schlägt Saphiras Skelett immer und immer wieder mit einer großen Axt>

Linus: Verdammt! Dein Skelett ist sehr mächtig!

Evelyn: Danke, knuddeliger Hamster! Aber ihr Skelett ist ziemlich schwach ...

<Saphira is grinning>

Saphira: You know what you have to do!

<Behold! Saphira's skeleton is brandishing its sword around in circles very fast>

Evelyn: Does it want to fly away?

<Evelyn is laughing. Suddenly, the sword of Saphira's skeleton has changed. It is no longer made of steel but of fire>

Saphira: Attack!

<Saphira's skeleton has just hit Evelyn's skeleton, but it's still standing>

Evelyn: Not even a scratch! Oh man, that's so boring to fight against you, Saphira!

Saphira: Are you sure?

<Behold! Evelyn's skeleton is turning to her with his eyes turned red>

<Saphira grinst>

Saphira: Du weißt, was du zu tun hast!

<Siehe! Saphiras Skelett schwingt sein Schwert sehr schnell im Kreis>

Evelyn: Will es davonfliegen?

<Evelyn lacht. Plötzlich hat sich das Schwert von Saphiras Skelett verändert. Es ist nicht mehr aus Stahl, sondern aus Feuer>

Saphira: Attacke!

<Saphiras Skelett hat gerade Evelyns Skelett getroffen, aber es steht noch immer>

Evelyn: Nicht einmal ein Kratzer! Oh Mann, es ist so langweilig, gegen dich zu kämpfen, Saphira!

Saphira: Bist du sicher?

<Siehe! Evelyns Skelett dreht sich mit rot gewordenen Augen zu ihr>

Evelyn: What are you doing?! Hit Saphira's skeleton with your damn axe!

Linus: Your skeleton doesn't look very friendly, Evelyn!

Evelyn: Damn!

<Evelyn's skeleton has just tried to hit her with its axe>

Evelyn: What are you doing?! Help me, please! I can't control it!

<Saphira's skeleton ran towards Evelyn's skeleton, jumped, and hit Evelyn's skeleton with its sword shortly before it had reached the ground. Now Evelyn's skeleton is lying on the ground>

Linus: It's defeated! Saphira has won! I knew that you'd win, Saphira!

Saphira: Thank you, Linus!

<Saphira is smiling>

Evelyn: Was tust du?! Schlag Saphiras Skelett mit deiner verdammten Axt!

Linus: Dein Skelett sieht nicht sehr freundlich aus, Evelyn!

Evelyn: Verdammt!

<Evelyns Skelett hat gerade versucht, sie mit seiner Axt zu schlagen>

Evelyn: Was tust du?! Helft mir, bitte! Ich kann es nicht kontrollieren!

<Saphiras Skelett rannte auf Evelyns Skelett zu, sprang und schlug Evelyns Skelett mit seinem Schwert, kurz bevor es den Boden erreicht hatte. Nun liegt Evelyns Skelett auf dem Boden>

Linus: Es ist besiegt! Saphira hat gewonnen! Ich wusste, du würdest gewinnen, Saphira!

Saphira: Danke, Linus!

<Saphira lächelt>

Evelyn: Well … I've lost … But I'd like to say thank you, Saphira. Your skeleton … YOU have just saved me … Without your help, I could have died ...

Saphira: It was nothing!

Linus: Hey, let's be friends! Who wants to hug and kiss me first?

<Saphira and Evelyn are laughing>

Evelyn: Nun … ich habe verloren … Aber ich möchte dir Danke sagen, Saphira. Dein Skelett … DU hast mich gerade gerettet … Ohne deine Hilfe hätte ich sterben können ...

Saphira: Nicht der Rede wert!

Linus: Hey, lasst uns Freunde sein! Wer möchte mich zuerst knuddeln?

<Saphira und Evelyn lachen>

16 The Queen's Important Package

<It's a beautiful evening in autumn. Saphira and Linus are talking about spells that are important to defeat demons and devils. Suddenly, someone has knocked on the door>

Saphira: One moment, please! I'm coming!

<Saphira has just opened the door>

Reinhard: I'm sorry for disturbing you, but the Queen herself gave me the order to ask you for a favour.

<Linus has just run to the door>

Linus: The Queen?! That's interesting!

<Now Saphira is bowing to Reinhard>

Saphira: It's an honour for us to serve the Queen.

<Linus is grinning while biting into his little piece of cake>

Reinhard: Alright! So, please listen to me.

16 Der Königin wichtiges Paket

<Es ist ein schöner Abend im Herbst. Saphira und Linus unterhalten sich gerade über Zauber, die wichtig für das Besiegen von Dämonen und Teufeln sind. Plötzlich hat jemand an die Tür geklopft>

Saphira: Einen Moment, bitte! Ich komme!

<Saphira hat gerade die Tür geöffnet>

Reinhard: Es tut mir Leid, euch zu stören, aber die Königin persönlich befahl mir, euch um einen Gefallen zu bitten.

<Linus ist gerade zur Tür gerannt>

Linus: Die Königin?! Das ist interessant!

<Nun verbeugt sich Saphira vor Reinhard>

Saphira: Es ist uns eine Ehre, der Königin zu dienen.

<Linus grinst, während er in sein kleines Tortenstück beißt>

Reinhard: Alles klar! Also, bitte hört mir zu!

Saphira: Sure!

Reinhard: It's very urgent that you go to the merchant called 'Clever Charlton Canter' and pick up a package for the Queen ...

Linus: Ah, I know that guy! He used to sell me delicious candy when I was young … Aaaah, I loved them and –

Saphira: Hush!

Reinhard: Well, as I said, the Queen needs that package very urgently. So, please go there as soon as possible.

Linus: Saphira, let's go there right away!

Saphira: Yes!

<Saphira has taken her magic wand>

Reinhard: Thank you so much! As soon as you've picked up the package, bring it to me, please. I'll be waiting in front of the palace.

Saphira: Ok! See you!

Saphira: Sicher!

Reinhard: Es ist sehr dringlich, dass ihr zu einem Händler namens „Clever Charlton Canter" geht und ein Paket für die Königin abholt ...

Linus: Ah, ich kenne diesen Typ! Er verkaufte mir damals köstliche Süßigkeiten, als ich jung war ... Aaaah, ich liebte sie und –

Saphira: Psst!

Reinhard: Nun, wie ich gesagt habe, die Königin braucht das Paket sehr dringend. Also, geht dort bitte so bald wie möglich hin.

Linus: Saphira, lass uns sofort dorthin gehen!

Saphira: Ja!

<Saphira hat ihren Zauberstab genommen>

Reinhard: Ich danke euch so sehr! Sobald ihr das Paket abgeholt habt, bringt es bitte zu mir. Ich werde vor dem Palast warten.

Saphira: Ok! Bis dann!

<Saphira and Linus have just arrived at Clever Charlton Canter's Shop >

Clever Charlton Canter: Ah, Linus, it's been a while ...

Linus: Yes! Do you still have some of that delicious candy?

<Saphira is rolling her eyes>

Saphira: Shut up, Linus! We've got a very important and very urgent quest to fulfill!

<Linus is smiling>

Linus: I'm sorry ...

Clever Charlton Canter: I see. You've come here to pick up the special package for the Queen?

Saphira: That's right.

Clever Charlton Canter: Here you are; please take care of it. It contains a VERY important thing!

<Saphira und Linus sind gerade in Clever Charlton Canters Geschäft angekommen>

Clever Charlton Canter: Ah, Linus, es ist eine Weile her ...

Linus: Ja! Hast du noch immer die köstlichen Süßigkeiten?

<Saphira verdreht die Augen>

Saphira: Halt die Klappe, Linus! Wir haben eine sehr wichtige und sehr dringliche Quest zu erledigen!

<Linus lächelt>

Linus: Tut mir leid ...

Clever Charlton Canter: Verstehe. Ihr seid hierher gekommen, um das besondere Paket für die Königin abzuholen?

Saphira: Das ist richtig.

Clever Charlton Canter: Hier, bitte passt darauf auf. Es beinhaltet etwas SEHR Wichtiges!

Linus: Sure, we'll be careful.

Saphira: Thank you! Goodbye!

Clever Charlton Canter: Bye!

<Saphira and Linus are on the way to the palace. Behold! Three unkempt men are walking towards them>

Linus: Out of the way, please! We've got a very important package for the Queen.

<The three men are laughing now>

First Man: You ain't going nowhere with that thing!

Third Man: That's right! We'll snatch it away from you two idiots!

Second Man: …

Saphira: We won't let you take it! Keep your dirty hands away from it!

<The men have just grabbed their swords>

Linus: Sicher, wir werden vorsichtig sein.

Saphira: Danke! Auf Wiedersehen!

Clever Charlton Canter: Tschüss!

<Saphira und Linus sind auf dem Weg zum Palast. Siehe da! Drei ungepflegte Männer laufen auf sie zu>

Linus: Aus dem Weg, bitte! Wir haben ein sehr wichtiges Paket für die Königin.

<Die drei Männer lachen nun>

Erster Mann: Ihr geht mit dem Ding nirgendwo hin!

Dritter Mann: Das ist richtig! Wir werden es euch beiden Idioten entreißen!

Zweiter Mann: …

Saphira: Wir werden es euch nicht nehmen lassen! Haltet eure dreckigen Hände fern!

<Die Männer haben gerade ihre Schwerter ergriffen>

First Man: Are you sure?

Third Man: Well, if you don't give us the package, we'll take it from your corpses!

<Linus is laughing>

Linus: You damn fools! We'll send you to your creator in the blink of an eye!

<Now the men are running towards Saphira and Linus>

Saphira: Leave it to me, Linus. I'm happy to try out my recently learned lightning spell!

Linus: Ok!

<Linus has just taken a snack out of his pocket>

Saphira: Dazzling lightning appear and shock those three men!

Erster Mann: Seid ihr sicher?

Dritter Mann: Nun, wenn ihr uns das Paket nicht gebt, dann werden wir es von euren Leichen nehmen!

<Linus lacht>

Linus: Ihr verdammten Narren! Wir werden euch in einem Wimpernschlag zu eurem Schöpfer schicken!

<Jetzt rennen die Männer auf Saphira und Linus zu>

Saphira: Überlass es mir, Linus. Ich freue mich darüber, meinen kürzlich gelernten Blitzzauber auszuprobieren!

Linus: Ok!

<Linus hat gerade einen Snack aus seiner Tasche geholt>

Saphira: Blendender Blitz erscheine und schocke jene drei Männer!

<Just after saying that, a dazzling blueish lightning appeared and shocked all three men. They were screaming loudly. Now all three men are lying on the ground, twisting in pain>

First Man: You've won! We give up!

Third Man: Yes, please forgive us!

Second Man: …

Saphira: Ok, Linus, the show's over! Let's take this package to Reinhard!

Linus: Let's go!

<Now Saphira and Linus are standing in front of Reinhard>

Reinhard: Ah, you are back! You've been pretty quick, I must say.

Linus: Thank you, but we've just done our job ...

<Nachdem sie dies gesagt hatte, erschien ein blendender bläulicher Blitz und schockte alle drei Männer. Sie schrien laut. Nun, liegen alle drei Männer auf dem Boden und krümmen sich vor Schmerzen>

Erster Mann: Ihr habt gewonnen! Wir geben auf!

Dritter Mann: Ja, bitte vergebt uns!

Zweiter Mann: …

Saphira: Ok, Linus, die Vorstellung ist vorbei! Lass uns dieses Paket zu Reinhard bringen!

Linus: Auf geht's!

<Nun stehen Saphira und Linus vor Reinhard>

Reinhard: Ah, ihr seid zurück! Ihr seid recht schnell gewesen, muss ich sagen.

Linus: Danke, aber wir haben nur unseren Job gemacht …

<Saphira is bowing to Reinhard while giving him the package>

Saphira: Here, the package.

Reinhard: Thank you so much! The Queen will give you a present for your help for sure. Stay here, please. I'll be back in a few minutes.

<Now Reinhard is running into the palace>

Reinhard: Your Majesty! Your Majesty! Here's your super-soft toilet paper!

<Saphira verneigt sich vor Reinhard, während sie ihm das Paket überreicht>

Saphira: Hier, das Paket.

Reinhard: Ich danke euch so sehr! Die Königin wird euch bestimmt ein Geschenk für eure Hilfe geben. Bleibt bitte hier. Ich bin in ein paar Minuten zurück.

<Nun rennt Reinhard in den Palast>

Reinhard: Eure Majestät! Eure Majestät! Hier ist Euer super-softes Klopapier!

17 The Snowman Competition

<Saphira and Linus are playing in the garden. It has been snowing all week>

Saphira: It's fun to play in the snow, isn't it?

<Now Linus is making a snow angel>

Linus: Of course! I like it when it's cold outside because I've got dense fur that keeps me warm.

<Saphira is levitating a big snowball>

Saphira: I'm glad that it's winter now. In the summer time, you always complain about the warm weather that is unbearable!

<Linus is laughing>

Linus: Well, you might be right … But I'm happy, too, that it isn't summer time because I don't have to see you wearing your ugly bikini …

17 Der Schneemannwettbewerb

<Saphira und Linus spielen gerade im Garten. Es hat die ganze Woche durchgeschneit>

Saphira: Es macht Spaß im Schnee zu spielen, nicht wahr?

<Nun macht Linus einen Schneeengel>

Linus: Natürlich! Ich mag es, wenn es draußen kalt ist, weil ich ein dichtes Fell habe, das mich warm hält.

<Saphira lässt einen großen Schneeball schweben>

Saphira: Ich bin froh, dass es jetzt Winter ist. In der Sommerzeit beschwerst du dich immer über das warme Wetter, das ist unerträglich!

<Linus lacht>

Linus: Nun, vielleicht hast du recht … Aber ich bin auch froh, dass es nicht Sommer ist, weil ich dich nicht in deinem hässlichen Bikini sehen muss ...

<Saphira has just thrown the big snowball with her magic wand onto Linus>

Linus: Aaah, help me!

<Saphira is laughing. Suddenly, Reinhard has come and is standing next to her now>

Saphira: Oh, I haven't noticed you at all. I'm sorry!

<Saphira is bowing to Reinhard now>

Reinhard: No problem! I see you have fun here in the snow ...

Linus: Well, would you like to join us?

<Reinhard is laughing>

Reinhard: Thank you for your invitation, but no. I've come here to tell you that a snowman competition will take place tomorrow.

Saphira: Sounds nice! We'd like to participate, too!

Linus: Where does it take place?

<Saphira hat gerade den großen Schneeball mit ihrem Zauberstab auf Linus geworfen>

Linus: Aaah, helft mir!

<Saphira lacht. Plötzlich ist Reinhard gekommen und steht nun neben ihr>

Saphira: Oh, ich habe dich gar nicht bemerkt. Tut mir leid!

<Saphira verbeugt sich nun vor Reinhard>

Reinhard: Kein Problem! Ich sehe, ihr habt Spaß im Schnee.

Linus: Nun, möchtest du mitmachen?

<Reinhard lacht>

Reinhard: Danke für deine Einladung, aber nein. Ich bin zu euch gekommen, um euch zu sagen, dass morgen ein Schneemannwettbewerb stattfinden wird.

Saphira: Hört sich gut an! Wir möchten auch teilnehmen!

Linus: Wo findet er statt?

Reinhard: In the meadow next to the palace.

Linus: Ok, we'll come! See you tomorrow!

<It's the following day. Saphira and Linus have just arrived at the meadow>

Reinhard: I say thank you to all who have come here! The person whose snowman is the most beautiful will win a marvellous golden tea cup!

<Linus is rolling in the snow laughing>

Saphira: Hush!

Reinhard: Let's begin! Ready, steady, GO!

<Now everybody is trying to build the most beautiful snowman. Linus is still laughing while Saphira is building a female snowman>

Saphira: I hope I will win the tea cup because I enjoy drinking a good cup of tea every morning.

Reinhard: Auf der Wiese neben dem Palast.

Linus: Ok, wir kommen! Bis morgen!

<Es ist der folgende Tag. Saphira und Linus sind gerade auf der Wiese angekommen>

Reinhard: Ich danke allen, die hierher gekommen sind! Die Person, deren Schneemann der schönste ist, wird eine wundervolle goldene Teetasse gewinnen!

<Linus rollt sich lachend im Schnee>

Saphira: Psst!

Reinhard: Lasst uns beginnen! Auf die Plätze, fertig, LOS!

<Jetzt versucht jeder, den schönsten Schneemann zu bauen. Linus lacht noch immer, während Saphira einen weiblichen Schneemann baut>

Saphira: Ich hoffe, dass ich die Teetasse gewinnen werde, weil es mir Spaß macht, jeden Morgen eine Tasse Tee zu trinken.

<Linus is watching Saphira now>

Linus: Hey, I know how you could win this competition!

Saphira: Tell me, please!

Linus: Just use one of your spells to let your snowgirl, eh, snowwoman … your whatever this is look beautiful!

Saphira: Come on, Linus, that would be against the rules!

Linus: Who cares? It's the cup you want, right?

Saphira: Of course I'd like to win it, but I want to win it without cheating!

Linus: Cheating?! Hey, you are a wizard; it's your profession, right? So, you wouldn't be a cheater if you made use of it.

<Behold! Saphira is throwing a few snowballs at Linus>

<Linus schaut nun Saphira zu>

Linus: Hey, ich weiß, wie du diesen Wettbewerb gewinnen könntest!

Saphira: Sag es mir bitte!

Linus: Benutze einfach einen deiner Zauber, um dein Schneemädchen, äh, Schneefrau … dein, was auch immer das ist, schön aussehen zu lassen!

Saphira: Komm schon, Linus, das wäre gegen die Regeln!

Linus: Wen interessiert's? Was du willst, ist die Tasse, richtig?

Saphira: Natürlich, ich möchte sie gewinnen, aber ich möchte sie ohne zu schummeln gewinnen!

Linus: Schummeln?! Hey, du bist eine Zauberin; es ist dein Beruf, richtig? Also, du wärst keine Schummlerin, wenn du davon Gebrauch machen würdest.

<Siehe! Saphira wirft ein paar Schneebälle auf Linus>

Linus: Aaah!

Saphira: So, I think that should be fine … Yes … that's it!

Reinhard: Alright, everybody, the time is over! The Queen herself is going to judge your snowmen.

<The Queen has finally come to Saphira to judge her female snowman>

Queen: This is a very beautiful snowman – sorry, snowwoman.

Saphira: I'm very pleased to hear that from you, Your Majesty.

Queen: I've made a decision … Saphira has won this competition!

Linus: Wow! You have won!

Saphira: Yes, and WITHOUT cheating!

<Linus is smiling>

Linus: Aaah!

Saphira: So, ich denke, das sollte gut sein … Ja … das ist es!

Reinhard: In Ordnung, ihr alle, die Zeit ist vorüber! Die Königin persönlich wird nun eure Schneemänner beurteilen.

<Die Königin ist schließlich zu Saphira gekommen, um ihren weiblichen Schneemann zu beurteilen>

Königin: Das ist ein sehr schöner Schneemann – Verzeihung, Schneefrau.

Saphira: Ich bin sehr erfreut, das von euch zu hören, Eure Majestät.

Königin: Ich habe mich entschieden … Saphira hat diesen Wettbewerb gewonnen!

Linus: Wow! Du hast gewonnen!

Saphira: Ja, und OHNE zu schummeln!

<Linus lächelt>

18 Saphira and Linus Are Camping

<It's a warm evening in September. Saphira and Linus are camping near their house at a stream>

Saphira: Aaah, it's so nice here, isn't it?

Linus: Yes, but these mosquitoes flying around here are making me mad!

<Saphira is laughing>

Saphira: Don't worry! I don't think that they can sting through your fur.

<Now Linus is scratching himself>

Linus: Well, I think one of them has already stinged me! My bottom is itching an –

Saphira: Look! Over there's a white wolf!

<Linus has just jumped onto Saphira's shoulder>

Linus: I hope that it isn't going to attack us.

18 Saphira und Linus campen

<Es ist ein warmer Abend im September. Saphira und Linus campen gerade in der Nähe ihres Hauses an einem Fluss>

Saphira: Aaah, es ist so schön hier, nicht wahr?

Linus: Ja, aber diese Stechmücken, die hier herumfliegen, machen mich verrückt!

<Saphira lacht>

Saphira: Keine Sorge! Ich glaube nicht, dass sie durch dein Fell stechen können.

<Jetzt kratzt sich Linus>

Linus: Also, ich glaube, eine hat mich bereits gestochen! Mein Hintern juckt un –

Saphira: Schau! Dort vorne ist ein weißer Wolf!

<Linus ist gerade auf Saphiras Schulter gesprungen>

Linus: Ich hoffe, dass er nicht vorhat, uns anzugreifen.

Saphira: No, I don't think so. It seems to be pretty peaceful at the moment.

Linus: Yes, I think you're right.

\<Linus is smiling\>

Linus: Come on, let's eat and drink something!

Saphira: Here are some of my special muffins! I made them last night.

Linus: Ah, that's why it was smelling so delicious!

\<Now Linus is trying to put two muffins into his mouth at the same time\>

Saphira: Wait! That's dangerous!

\<Linus has already eaten both muffins\>

Linus: Wow! They taste soo good! Please give me some more!

Saphira: There's only one left ...

Saphira: Nein, ich glaube nicht. Er scheint im Moment ziemlich friedlich zu sein.

Linus: Ja, ich glaube, du hast recht.

<Linus lächelt>

Linus: Komm schon, lass uns etwas essen und trinken!

Saphira: Hier sind ein paar meiner besonderen Muffins! Ich habe sie letzte Nacht gemacht.

Linus: Ah, deshalb roch es so köstlich!

<Nun versucht Linus, zwei Muffins auf einmal in seinen Mund zu stopfen>

Saphira: Warte! Das ist gefährlich!

<Linus hat bereits beide Muffins gegessen>

Linus: Wow! Sie schmecken soo gut! Bitte gib mir ein paar weitere!

Saphira: Es ist nur noch einer übrig ...

Linus: Only one?!

<Now a cold wind is blowing>

Saphira: I-it's soo cold. I'm shivering!

Linus: Yes … yes, you're right. How's that possible? A few minutes ago, it was pretty warm!

Saphira: Over there! The white wolf is howling, and every time he does so, a frigid gust of wind is emitted.

Linus: I can't believe it! It's not a normal wolf.

<Suddenly, the wolf has disappeared>

Linus: Where is it now?

Saphira: I don't know, but I'm feeling pretty bad at the moment … I think something is going to happen very soon ...

<Behold! The sky is darkening and snow is falling>

Linus: Nur noch einer?!

<Nun weht ein kalter Wind>

Saphira: E-es ist so kalt. Ich zittere!

Linus: Ja … ja, du hast recht. Wie ist das möglich? Vor ein paar Minuten war es noch warm!

Saphira: Dort! Der weiße Wolf heult, und jedes Mal, wenn er es tut, wird ein eisiger Windhauch ausgestoßen.

Linus: Ich kann es nicht glauben! Er ist kein normaler Wolf.

<Plötzlich ist der Wolf verschwunden>

Linus: Wo ist er jetzt?

Saphira: Ich weiß es nicht, aber ich fühle mich gerade ziemlich schlecht … Ich denke, dass bald etwas geschehen wird ...

<Siehe! Der Himmel verdunkelt sich und Schnee fällt>

Saphira: What is happening? It's summer! Why is it snowing?!

Linus: I bet that the white wolf is causing this. I'll kick his butt!

<A strange voice can be heard>

Voice: Cold and heartless is this world … All inhabitants deserve punishment!

Saphira: Veni, calida aestas!

<Saphira has just cast her spell, and now a pillar of fire has appeared>

Saphira: I'll burn you – whoever you are!

<The voice is laughing now>

Voice: Damn little girl! I'll freeze you to death and eat you! I haven't had dinner yet, so I'm VERY hungry ...

<The voice has disappeared>

Saphira: Was geschieht hier? Es ist Sommer! Warum schneit es?!

Linus: Ich wette, dass der weiße Wolf dafür verantwortlich ist. Ich werde ihn in den Hintern treten!

<Man kann eine seltsame Stimme hören>

Stimme: Kalt und herzlos ist die Welt … Alle Bewohner verdienen eine Bestrafung!

Saphira: Veni, calida aestas!

<Saphira hat gerade ihren Zauber gewirkt und nun ist eine Säule aus Feuer erschienen>

Saphira: Ich werde dich verbrennen – wer auch immer du bist!

<Die Stimme lacht nun>

Stimme: Verdammtes kleines Mädchen! Ich werde dich einfrieren und essen! Ich habe noch nicht zu Abend gegessen, deshalb bin ich SEHR hungrig …

<Die Stimme ist verschwunden>

Linus: I don't have my warhammer with me, so I can't help you, Saphira.

Saphira: Don't worry! Everything is under control.

<Now Saphira is moving the pillar of fire with her magic wand to the sky. Behold! A wizard wearing a black robe has appeared on a hill with a white wolf by his side, just in front of Saphira and Linus>

Wizard: You people destroy nature and hunt my beloved wolves!

Saphira: There may be cruel people that do so, but Linus and I ... and so many other people don't do such things! So, please let us live in peace!

<The wizard is grinning now>

Wizard: Get them!

<While the white wolf is running towards Saphira and Linus, it's barking>

Saphira: This fire will bring you peace!

Linus: Ich habe meinen Kriegshammer nicht bei mir, also kann ich dir nicht helfen, Saphira.

Saphira: Keine Sorge, alles ist unter Kontrolle.

<Nun bewegt Saphira die Säule aus Feuer mit ihrem Zauberstab Richtung Himmel. Siehe! Ein Zauberer, der eine schwarze Robe trägt, ist auf einem Hügel mit einem weißen Wolf an seiner Seite erschienen, direkt vor Saphira und Linus>

Zauberer: Ihr Leute zerstört die Natur und jagt meine geliebten Wölfe!

Saphira: Es mag grausame Leute geben, die so etwas machen, aber Linus und ich ... und so viele andere Leute machen solche Dinge nicht! Also, bitte lass uns in Frieden leben!

<Der Zauberer grinst nun>

Zauberer: Schnapp sie dir!

<Während der weiße Wolf auf Saphira und Linus zurennt, bellt er>

Saphira: Dieses Feuer wird dir Frieden bringen!

<The mighty pillar of fire has turned into a wall of fire and is moving towards the wolf and the wizard now>

Wizard: Do you believe that your ridiculous wall of fire can defeat us?!

<The wizard is laughing>

Linus: Ha, try to defeat me, stinky old man!

<Behold! Linus is standing behind the wizard brandishing a thick branch>

Wizard: I'll mash you, hamster!

<Linus is laughing while the wizard is lifting his right leg. Just as the wizard was moving his foot down, Linus hit him with the thick branch, and the wizard was flying through the air screaming>

Saphira: The white wolf is fleeing!

Linus: That's great!

<Die mächtige Säule aus Feuer ist eine Wand aus Feuer geworden und bewegt sich nun auf den Wolf und den Zauberer zu>

Zauberer: Glaubst du, dass deine lächerliche Wand aus Feuer uns besiegen kann?!

<Der Zauberer lacht>

Linus: Ha, versuch mich zu besiegen, stinkender alter Mann!

<Siehe! Linus steht hinter dem Zauberer, einen dicken Ast schwingend>

Zauberer: Ich werde dich zerquetschen, Hamster!

<Linus lacht, während der Zauberer sein rechtes Bein hebt. Gerade als der Zauberer sein Bein nach unten bewegte, schlug Linus ihn mit dem dicken Ast und der Zauberer flog schreiend durch die Luft>

Saphira: Der weiße Wolf ergreift die Flucht!

Linus: Das ist großartig!

<The sky is as it had been before the wolf started to howl, and it has just stopped snowing>

Saphira: Who was that wizard?

Linus: I don't know. I haven't seen him before ... Well, now that he's gone, let's eat the remaining muffin together!

<Saphira is laughing>

<Der Himmel ist wieder wie er gewesen war, bevor der Wolf zu heulen begann, und es hat gerade aufgehört zu schneien>

Saphira: Wer war jener Zauberer?

Linus: Ich weiß nicht. Ich habe ihn noch nie zuvor gesehen ... Nun, da er fort ist, lass uns gemeinsam den übriggebliebenen Muffin essen!

<Saphira lacht>

19 Into the Empire of Inias?!

<Saphira and Linus are hearing screaming people>

Saphira: Let's go out and check what is happening!

Linus: Yes, let's go!

Saphira: Oh no! Look, over there are zombies and other creatures!

Linus: From where could they have come? I don't think that a necromancer has reanimated the dead from the nearby cemetery …

Saphira: I agree. Those creatures seem different …

<Behold! Reinhard is running towards Saphira and Linus>

Reinhard: Saphira, Linus! Please help us! We are being attacked by skeletons, zombies, and some unknown creatures! They are all coming out of a huge portal on the marketplace! Please go there and try to defeat them!

19 Ins Reich des Inias?!

<Saphira und Linus hören gerade schreiende Leute>

Saphira: Lass uns nach draußen gehen und schauen, was geschieht!

Linus: Ja, lass uns gehen!

Saphira: Oh nein! Schau, dort drüben sind Zombies und andere Kreaturen!

Linus: Woher könnten sie gekommen sein? Ich glaube nicht, dass ein Nekromant die Toten des nahegelegenen Friedhofs wiederbelebt hat …

Saphira: Ich stimme zu. Diese Kreaturen sehen anders aus …

<Siehe! Reinhard rennt auf Saphira und Linus zu>

Reinhard: Saphira, Linus! Bitte helft uns! Wir werden von Skeletten, Zombies und ein paar unbekannten Kreaturen angegriffen! Sie kommen alle aus einem großen Portal auf dem Marktplatz heraus! Bitte geht dorthin und versucht sie zu besiegen!

Linus: Yeah! I'm happy to crush some skulls!

<Linus is laughing>

Saphira: We'll do our best to defeat as many monsters as we can! Let's go, Linus!

<Saphira and Linus have just come to the huge portal>

Saphira: Finally, I can try out some of my spells that ban undead creatures.

<Now Saphira is casting some spells while Linus is jumping from one skeleton to another and crushing their skulls>

Linus: Haha, that's fun!

<Behold! Something is sucking Saphira into the portal>

Saphira: Help me! I'm being sucked into the portal!

Linus: Yeah! Ich freue mich, dass ich ein paar Schädel zertrümmern kann!

<Linus lacht>

Saphira: Wir werden unser Bestes geben, so viele Monster wie wir können zu besiegen! Lass uns gehen, Linus!

<Saphira und Linus sind gerade zum großen Portal gekommen>

Saphira: Endlich kann ich ein paar meiner Zauber, die untote Kreaturen verbannen können, ausprobieren.

<Jetzt wirkt Saphira verschiedene Zauber, während Linus von einem Skelett zum anderen springt und ihre Schädel zertrümmert>

Linus: Haha, das macht Spaß!

<Schau! Etwas saugt Saphira in das Portal>

Saphira: Helft mir! Ich werde in das Portal gesogen!

<Now Linus and some of the town guards are running to Saphira>

Linus: We'll help you!

Saphira: Aaah!

<Saphira has just been sucked into the portal>

Linus: Saphira! … I must go into the portal, too! You keep on defeating the creatures!

A Town Guard: Of course, good luck!

Linus: Everything is dark … I can't even see my paws …

Saphira: Linus?

Linus: Saphira? Where are you? I can't see anything!

Saphira: Wait a moment; I'll teleport you to the place where I am.

Linus: Ok!

<Nun rennen Linus und ein paar der Stadtwachen zu Saphira>

Linus: Wir helfen dir!

Saphira: Aaah!

<Saphira ist gerade in das Portal gesogen worden>

Linus: Saphira! ... Ich muss auch in das Portal gehen! Ihr fahrt damit fort, die Kreaturen zu besiegen!

Eine Stadtwache: Natürlich, viel Glück!

Linus: Alles ist dunkel … Ich kann nicht einmal meine Pfoten sehen …

Saphira: Linus?

Linus: Saphira? Wo bist du? Ich kann überhaupt nichts sehen!

Saphira: Warte kurz; ich teleportiere dich an den Ort, an dem ich mich befinde.

Linus: Ok!

<Saphira has just teleported Linus to her left shoulder>

Saphira: Are you ok?

Linus: Yes, thank you! Where are we?

Saphira: This is the Empire of Inias, an undead lord. I'm pretty sure because I've read about his empire in a book recently. Three hundred years ago, Inias attacked our beautiful town for the first time, but our Queen could defeat him. Since then, nobody has ever heard of him again. I don't think tha –

Inias: That's all true, what you said. But THIS time I'll get the Queen's magic necklace for sure …

Linus: The necklace? Why do you want it?

Inias: A talking hamster?

<Inias is laughing now. Saphira has just summoned a powerful black demon>

<Saphira hat gerade Linus auf ihre linke Schulter teleportiert>

Saphira: Bist du in Ordnung?

Linus: Ja, danke! Wo sind wir?

Saphira: Das ist das Reich von Inias, einem untoten Herrscher. Ich bin mir ziemlich sicher, weil ich kürzlich in einem Buch über sein Reich gelesen habe. Vor dreihundert Jahren griff Inias unsere schöne Stadt das erste Mal an, aber unsere Königin konnte ihn besiegen. Seit jener Zeit hat niemand mehr von ihm gehört. Ich glaube nicht, da –

Inias: Es ist alles wahr, was du gesagt hast. Aber DIESES Mal werde ich die magische Halskette der Königin bekommen …

Linus: Die Halskette? Warum willst du sie?

Inias: Ein sprechender Hamster?

<Inias lacht nun. Saphira hat gerade einen mächtigen schwarzen Dämon beschworen>

Linus: Time to crush one more skull!

<Behold! Linus is running towards Inias, even though he is throwing green fireballs. Saphira and the black demon are casting different spells>

Inias: Oh, you are stronger than I thought!

<Now Linus is hitting Inias over and over again with his warhammer while Saphira's black demon is trying to confuse him so that all of his green fireballs neither hit Linus nor Saphira>

Inias: I-I'll turn you … into zombies … I …

Saphira: Time to ban you forever!

<Behold, a bright, yellow ray of light is being emitted from the demon's hand and Saphira's magic wand>

Inias: Aaah …

<The two rays have just hit Inias>

Linus: Zeit, einen weiteren Schädel zu zertrümmern!

<Siehe! Linus rennt auf Inias zu, obwohl er grüne Feuerbälle wirft. Saphira und der schwarze Dämon wirken verschiedene Zauber>

Inias: Oh, ihr seid stärker, als ich dachte!

<Jetzt schlägt Linus Inias immer wieder mit seinem Kriegshammer, während Saphiras schwarzer Dämon versucht, ihn zu verwirren, sodass all seine grünen Feuerbälle weder Linus noch Saphira treffen>

Inias: I-ich werde euch … in Zombies … Ich …

Saphira: Zeit, dich für immer zu verbannen!

<Siehe, ein heller, gelber Lichtstrahl wird von der Hand des Dämons und Saphiras Zauberstab abgegeben>

Inias: Aaah …

<Die beiden Strahlen haben gerade Inias getroffen>

Linus:... Where am I? Saphira? Where are you?

<Saphira is smiling>

Saphira: I'm next to you ... Everything is fine ... We've banned Inias. All creatures and the portal are gone. After the rays had hit him, we were teleported to the marketplace. After a few minutes, Reinhard came and brought us to a healer – this is where we are now.

Linus: Thank you for your help, Reinhard ... If you don't mind, I'd like to eat something delicious.

<Saphira and Reinhard are laughing>

Linus:...Wo bin ich? Saphira? Wo bist du?

<Saphira lächelt>

Saphira: Ich bin neben dir ... Alles ist gut ... Wir haben Inias verbannt. Alle Kreaturen und das Portal sind fort. Nachdem die Strahlen ihn getroffen hatten, wurden wir auf den Marktplatz teleportiert. Nach ein paar Minuten kam Reinhard und brachte uns zu einem Heiler – das ist der Ort, wo wir jetzt sind.

Linus: Danke für deine Hilfe, Reinhard ... Wenn es dir nichts ausmacht, würde ich gerne etwas Köstliches essen.

<Saphira und Reinhard lachen>

20 The Shadow Cat of the Queen

<Linus is repairing his old warhammer while Saphira is working in her laboratory. Now Linus notices a strange shadow in front of the window>

Linus: Hey, what's that? That shadow can't be caused by an object because there's no object near the window ... Hm, I think I should open it and see what it is ...

<Linus has jumped onto the window-sill>

Linus: It's gone! Where's that shadow?!

<Now Saphira is coming into the room>

Saphira: What's the matter, Linus?

<Linus is turning to Saphira>

Linus: There has been a strange shadow in front of this window – but now it's gone ...

20 Die Schattenkatze der Königin

<Linus repariert gerade seinen alten Kriegshammer, während Saphira in ihrem Laboratorium arbeitet. Jetzt bemerkt Linus einen seltsamen Schatten vor dem Fenster>

Linus: Hey, was ist das? Jener Schatten da kann von keinem Objekt verursacht werden, weil es kein Objekt in der Nähe des Fensters gibt ... Hm, ich denke, ich sollte es öffnen und schauen, was es ist ...

<Linus ist auf das Fensterbrett gesprungen>

Linus: Er ist fort! Wo ist der Schatten?!

<Jetzt kommt Saphira in das Zimmer>

Saphira: Was ist los, Linus?

<Linus dreht sich zu Saphira>

Linus: Es hat sich ein seltsamer Schatten vor diesem Fenster befunden – aber nun ist er fort ...

<Saphira is holding her chin with her right hand while thinking of that strange shadow>

Saphira: Hm, that's mysterious for sure ...

Linus: Could it have been a ghost?

Saphira: Well, ghosts usually show up when it's night.

Linus: Oh, you're right ...

<Suddenly, the vase that has been standing on the sideboard for many years has just fallen down>

Saphira: Oh no, the beautiful vase! Why has it fallen down the sideboard? Nobody had touched it ...

Linus: Look! On the chair next to the sideboard is the shadow!

<After Saphira had looked at the shadow, it has turned into a black cat>

<Saphira hält sich ihr Kinn mit ihrer rechten Hand, während sie über den seltsamen Schatten nachdenkt>

Saphira: Hm, das ist auf jeden Fall mysteriös ...

Linus: Könnte es ein Geist gewesen sein?

Saphira: Nun, Geister zeigen sich gewöhnlich in der Nacht.

Linus: Oh, du hast recht ...

<Plötzlich ist die Vase, die seit vielen Jahren auf der Anrichte gestanden hat, hinuntergefallen>

Saphira: Oh nein, die schöne Vase! Warum ist sie von der Anrichte gefallen? Niemand hatte sie berührt ...

Linus: Schau! Auf dem Stuhl neben der Anrichte ist der Schatten!

<Nachdem Saphira den Schatten angeschaut hatte, hat er sich in eine schwarze Katze verwandelt>

Saphira: Now I understand! This is a so called 'Shadow Cat'! Shadow Cats are magic creatures that are able to turn their appearance into a shadow as well as a real cat.

Linus: Wow, that's pretty impressive!

Saphira: Indeed, but Shadow Cats usually avoid places where humans live. Why is it here?

Linus: Probably it likes hamsters!

<Saphira is rolling her eyes>

Saphira: Of course ...

Linus: Do you smell that? It smells like urine ...

<Saphira is laughing>

Saphira: It seems that it has just –

Linus: Stop, I know! I can't believe it! It has just gone through the wall!

Saphira: Nun verstehe ich! Das ist eine sogenannte „Schattenkatze"! Schattenkatzen sind magische Kreaturen, die ihr Aussehen sowohl in einen Schatten als auch in eine reale Katze verwandeln können.

Linus: Wow, das ist ziemlich beeindruckend!

Saphira: In der Tat, aber gewöhnlich meiden Schattenkatzen Orte, an denen Menschen leben. Warum ist sie hier?

Linus: Wahrscheinlich mag sie Hamster!

<Saphira verdreht die Augen>

Saphira: Natürlich ...

Linus: Riechst du das? Es riecht nach Urin ...

<Saphira lacht>

Saphira: Es scheint, dass sie gerade –

Linus: Stopp, ich weiß! Ich kann es nicht glauben! Sie ist gerade durch die Wand gegangen!

Saphira: Wow! I've always thought that they couldn't do this.

Linus: Come on, let's follow it and see to whom it belongs!

Saphira: Ok, let's go!

<Saphira and Linus have followed the Shadow Cat up to the palace>

Linus: Interesting … I bet that it belongs to the Queen.

Saphira: Yes, I think so, too. Well, but we can't confirm our suggestion, because we won't get permission to enter the palace.

Linus: What a pity … Hm … Hey, I've got an idea!

Saphira: Oh dear ...

Linus: I know that the small window of the Queen's room is usually open.

Saphira: Wow! Ich habe immer gedacht, dass sie das nicht könnten.

Linus: Komm schon, lass uns ihr folgen und schauen, zu wem sie gehört!

Saphira: Ok, lass uns gehen!

<Saphira und Linus sind der Schattenkatze bis zum Palast gefolgt>

Linus: Interessant ... Ich wette, dass sie zur Königin gehört.

Saphira: Ja, das denke ich auch. Nun, aber wir können unsere Vermutung nicht bestätigen, weil wir nicht die Erlaubnis bekommen werden, in den Palast zu gehen.

Linus: Wie schade … Hm … Hey, ich habe eine Idee!

Saphira: Oje ...

Linus: Ich weiß, dass das kleine Fenster des Zimmers der Königin gewöhnlich offen ist.

Saphira: That's not a window of her room but the window of her bathroom.

Linus: Oh ... That doesn't matter. I'll try to climb up there and get into the bathroom. Then, I'll try to find the Shadow Cat.

Saphira: Are you sure? It sounds dangerous!

Linus: Don't worry, I'll make it for sure!

Saphira: Ok, but I'll be waiting for you at home. I don't want to be led away by the guards.

Linus: Ok, I'm fine with that; see you!

<Linus has reached the window>

Linus: Oh dear ... She's taking a bath at the moment – what should I do?

<The Queen is singing funny songs, and Linus can't hold back from laughing>

Queen: What was that?

Saphira: Das ist kein Fenster ihres Zimmers, sondern von ihrem Badezimmer.

Linus: Oh ... Das macht nichts. Ich werde versuchen, hinaufzuklettern und in das Badezimmer zu gelangen. Dann werde ich versuchen, die Schattenkatze zu finden.

Saphira: Bist du sicher? Es klingt gefährlich!

Linus: Keine Sorge, ich werde es sicher schaffen!

Saphira: Ok, aber ich werde zu Hause auf dich warten. Ich will nicht von den Wachen abgeführt werden.

Linus: Ok, das ist in Ordnung für mich; bis dann!

<Linus hat das Fenster erreicht>

Linus: Oje ... Sie badet gerade – was soll ich tun?

<Die Königin singt lustige Lieder und Linus kann es nicht unterlassen, zu lachen>

Königin: Was war das?

<Behold! Linus is falling into the bathtub>

Queen: Aaaah!

<The Queen has just grabbed Linus>

Queen: Linus?! What are you doing here?

<Linus is blushing>

Linus: I'm so sorry, Your Majesty! Saphira and I are so curious if the Shadow Cat that we've seen is yours ...

<The Queen is laughing>

Queen: Yes, it belongs to me. My sister gave it to me as a present. I love Shadow Cats. Please excuse my little kitty for disturbing you.

Linus: N-no problem, Your Majesty. Well, may I go back home now and tell Saphira the news?

<Siehe! Linus fällt in die Badewanne>

Königin: Aaaah!

<Die Königin hat gerade Linus geschnappt>

Königin: Linus?! Was machst du hier?

<Linus errötet>

Linus: Es tut mir so leid, Eure Majestät! Saphira und ich sind so neugierig darauf, ob die Schattenkatze, die wir gesehen haben, Euch gehört ...

<Die Königin lacht>

Königin: Ja, sie gehört zu mir. Meine Schwester hat sie mir geschenkt. Ich liebe Schattenkatzen. Bitte entschuldige, dass mein kleines Kätzchen euch belästigt hat.

Linus: K-kein Problem, Eure Majestät. Nun, darf ich jetzt nach Hause gehen und Saphira die Neuigkeiten berichten?

Queen: Sure. But next time you'd like to know something from me, ask one of the guards for an audience with me, please. Alright?

Linus: Of course, Your Majesty! Goodbye!

Königin: Sicher. Aber das nächste Mal, wenn ihr etwas von mir wissen möchtet, bittet einen der Wächter um eine Audienz mit mir, in Ordnung?

Linus: Natürlich, Eure Majestät! Auf Wiedersehen!

Übungen

1. Setze das passende Wort ein:
who, day, too, magic, early, well

1.1 It's ... in the morning. Linus is brushing his teeth.

1.2 Saphira is very interested in ...

1.3 Do you know ... Reinhard is?

1.4 The Queen can play the flute very ...

1.5 No, that's ... much ice cream for this little girl.

1.6 Saphira and Linus went to 'Vinegar Castle' the other ...

2. Übersetze ins Deutsche

2.1 Saphira has improved her fighting style.

2.2 Reinhard used to go sledging when he was young.

2.3 Linus won't give his warhammer to a stranger.

2.4 Saphira and Linus have been busy this week.

2.5 The Queen was reading a funny book in the afternoon.

2.6 Saphira usually doesn't put on make-up.

2.7 The Queen will be on holiday from June until August.

2.8 Saphira said that she had seen a black spider in her room.

2.9 Linus asked a friend to help him decorate the garden for Saphira's birthday.

2.10 Saphira wasn't at home when I visited Linus in spring.

2.11 Here is your pink pair of briefs, Linus!

2.12 I'm sorry, but I do not know a wizard called Tusiosius.

3. Bilde das „Futur Perfect"

3.1 Saphira (to eat) by 10 o'clock.

3.2 Linus (to write) a letter to his mum before she comes to visit him.

3.3 Reinhard (to buy) new shoes for the Queen before she has got up.

3.4 Saphira and Linus (to drink) all orange juice by this evening.

3.5 Saphira (to come back) before night falls.

4. Übersetze ins Deutsche

4.1 What a wonderful crystal! It's sparkling so nicely!

4.2 A legendary treasure is said to be hidden in that castle.

4.3 Linus, come here, please! A letter from your father has arrived!

4.4 Don't call me a liar! I did see the Queen wearing a red bikini when I was 15 years old!

4.5 What the hell are you talking about?!

4.6 Look up to the sky, and you'll see three dragons fighting against each other when the time has come.

4.7 Oh, I didn't realize that it was you who was swimming in the lake last night.

4.8 I know, but please be more careful from now on.

4.9 Get me a cool drink, please. I'm thirsty.

5. *Bringe die Sätze in die richtige Reihenfolge*

5.1 the house?/ When / Linus / leave / did

5.2 years / ago, / Two hundred / was / an eclipse of the sun. / there

5.3 I think, / The more / the more / I get confused.

5.4 out / Get / Linus! / of / bed, / your

5.5 Why / you / have / Saphira? / scolded

5.6 orcs! / Aaaah, / there / over / are / five /

6. *Übersetze ins Englische*

6.1 Es besteht keine Notwendigkeit, einen neuen Zauber anzuwenden.

6.2 Gibt es in der „Essigburg" ein altes Buch?

6.3 Nein, ich habe niemanden gesehen, der einen grünen Hut trug.

6.4 Es gibt vier alte weise Männer: Irinas, Salaryna, Telarius, Sonorius.

6.5 Gestern funkelten die Sterne, während ich in der Hängematte lag.

6.6 Geh sofort zur Königin; es ist dringend!

6.7 Kannst du den Thron der Königin sehen?

6.8 Er sagte, er habe dich mit Reinhard zum Marktplatz gehen sehen.

7. Bilde den Komparativ und Superlativ

7.1 angry

7.2 funny

7.3 large

7.4 small

7.5 great

7.6 cold

7.7 hot

7.8 soft

7.9 weak

7.10 powerful

7.11 clear

7.12 thick

8. Füge das passende Fragewort ein:
what, how, who, when

8.1 ... is that little girl caressing the white cat?

- That's Reinhard's daughter, Sigrist.

8.2 ... did Saphira start to study magic?

- I don't know exactly, but it is surely several years ago.

8.3 ... do you write a spell role?

- Ah, that's not that hard. Here, I'll show you.

8.4 ... is that thing on the table?

- Ah, that's a little cauldron.

8.5 ... long has she been in her laboratory?
- She's been there for 6 hours now.

9. Gib die Sätze in „Reported Speech" wieder

9.1 Saphira: Don't touch this bottle! It contains a dangerous fluid!

9.2 Linus: Dream on! You aren't as good as I am!

9.3 The Queen: Never go there again! There are evil fairies in the forest at night!

9.4 Reinhard: Would you please help me with this?

9.5 An Old Man: I've never seen a talking hamster.

9.6 Linus: Saphira will have learned these spells by the end of this week.

9.7 Reinhard: Ok, I'll be waiting for you; please don't be late.

9.8 Saphira: I've known him for many years.

9.9 Linus: If you don't mind, I'll call Saphira.

9.10 Linus: Yes, this would help me a lot.

10. Übersetze ins Englische

10.1 Heute habe ich bereits zehn neue Zauber gelernt.

10.2 Hast du gestern auch die vielen Sternschnuppen gesehen?

10.3 Ich hätte lieber eine neue Robe.

10.4 Niemals wieder werde ich dir ein Geheimnis anvertrauen!

10.5 In der Tat, ich bin auf diesem Gebiet der Magie sehr bewandert.

10.6 Gib mir bitte das Glas Wasser.

10.7 Ich werde nun nach dem magischen Ring fragen.

10.8 Sehr gut, ich brauche nur noch eine einzige Zutat!

11. Bilde das „Simple Present" der folgenden Verben und füge sie in der richtigen Form in die Sätze ein

Verben: to build, to catch, to chase, to dream, to wake up, to laugh, to water

11.1 Saphira usually ... snowmen in winter.

11.2 Linus sometimes … the flowers in the morning.

11.3 The Queen always … at 6 o'clock.

11.4 Linus and Reinhard sometimes ... burglars.

11.5 Saphira and Linus often ... about each other.

11.6 Saphira ... a cold not very often.

11.7 Linus often ... of mountains made of cream.

12. Gib die Sätze in „Reported Speech" wieder

12.1 Saphira: Do you know where my magic wand is?

12.2 Linus: We are on a journey to find four magic crystals.

12.3 Reinhard: I understand – I wish you well.

12.4 The Queen: Try to find information about the recent strange happenings.

12.5 Saphira: A dragon is standing on the frozen lake.

12.6 Linus: I've got no more gold coins, sorry.

12.7 Saphira: I love reading books in the library.

12.8 Linus: My favourite toothbrush isn't at its usual place.

12.9 Reinhard: That was a beautiful evening yesterday.

12.10 The Queen: My new gloves have just arrived.

13. Übersetze ins Deutsche

13.1 Watch out! The stones are slippery!

13.2 This armour is resonably priced! I'd like to buy it!

13.3 I agree. I'll stay here and defeat the remaining monsters.

13.4 I think I've broken my arm. Please help me!

13.5 Two orcs are controlling the bridge!

14. Übersetze ins Englische

14.1 Saphira ist so süß, wenn sie lächelt.

14.2 Saphira und Linus müssen einen Bauernhof vor Dämonen beschützen.

14.3 Saphira ist bereits im Reich des Inias gewesen.

14.4 Linus wird bestimmt heute Abend am Kamin ein Buch seines Lieblingsschriftstellers lesen.

14.5 Drei Wochen sind bereits vergangen und wir haben noch immer keine Nachricht von der Königin der Elfen erhalten ...

15. Bilde das Adverb

15.1 strong

15.2 hard

15.3 heavy

15.4 clear

15.5 soft

15.6 urgent

16. Bilde das „Simple Past" und „Past Participle"

16.1 to grant

16.2 to offer

16.3 to cleanse

16.4 to bare

16.5 to water

16.6 to pour

16.7 to rain

16.8 to proof

16.9 to rescue

16.10 to heal

16.11 to save

16.12 to bring

17. Bilde Bedingungssätze vom Typ II

17.1 If I go there, I'll meet you.

17.2 If you know him, he will know you.

17.3 If there's a treasure, I want it.

17.4 If I insert this stone, the door will open!

17.5 If there's no more juice, I will ask Saphira to buy another bottle.

17.6 If Linus is not at home, Saphira will tell you.

17.7 If Saphira needs a new bottle, she will tell Linus.

18. Bringe die Sätze in die richtige Reihenfolge

18.1 a legendary spell role. / Saphira / didn't / see / while / she was looking for / a ghost

18.2 the enemy / Saphira and Linus / beloved town. / won't / let / capture / their

18.3 is / making / for / a sandwich / himself. / Linus

18.4 running / Saphira / across / the meadow. / is

18.5 when / Linus / came home. /had eaten / the whole cake / Saphira

18.6 are talking about / Reinhard and the Queen / next Sunday. / a funny play / that / will be performed

18.7 bandits / Four / a rich merchant. / have just robbed

18.8 don't / Time / think? / flies, / you /

19. Übersetze ins Deutsche

19.1 Where have you been for so long?

19.2 Welcome back home, my lovely sister!

19.3 After Saphira had finished her work in the laboratory, she went for a walk with Linus.

19.4 Can you imagine how brilliant that wizard must have been?

19.5 I've never heard of such a ridiculous story!

19.6 Maybe we'll see each other again ...

19.7 Death won't get us! Let's drink this potion and become immortal!

19.8 Out of my way! Don't dare cross my way again!

20. Übersetze ins Englische

20.1 Saphira will mit Reinhard über eine seltsame Kreatur, die sie in der Nähe der Stadt gesehen hat, sprechen.

20.2 Linus möchte gerne den Salat anmachen.

20.3 Saphira und Linus haben Tante Julica schon seit 5 Jahren nicht mehr gesehen.

20.4 Was ist so wichtig an diesem Zauber?

20.5 Möchtest du uns zur nächsten Taverne begleiten?

Lösungsschlüssel

1. Übung

1.1 early

1.2 magic

1.3 who

1.4 well

1.5 too

1.6 day

2. Übung

2.1 Saphira hat ihren Kampfstil verbessert.

2.2 Reinhard ging damals, als er jung war, Schlitten fahren.

2.3 Linus weigert sich, seinen Kriegshammer einem Fremden zu geben.

2.4 Saphira und Linus sind diese Woche beschäftigt gewesen.

2.5 Die Königin las am Nachmittag ein lustiges Buch.

2.6 Saphira schminkt sich gewöhnlich nicht.

2.7 Die Königin wird von Juni bis August im Urlaub sein.

2.8 Saphira sagte, sie habe eine schwarze Spinne in ihrem Zimmer gesehen.

2.9 Linus bat einen Freund darum, ihm beim Schmücken des Gartens für Saphiras Geburtstag zu helfen.

2.10 Saphira war nicht zuhause, als ich Linus im Frühling besuchte.

2.11 Hier ist deine rosa Unterhose, Linus!

2.12 Es tut mir leid, aber ich kenne keinen Zauberer namens Tusiosius.

3. Übung

3.1 will have eaten

3.2 will have written

3.3 will have bought

3.4 will have drunk

3.5 will have come back

4. Übung

4.1 Was für ein wunderschöner Kristall! Er funkelt so schön!

4.2 Es heißt, dass ein legendärer Schatz in jener Burg versteckt sei.

4.3 Linus, komm bitte her! Ein Brief von deinem Vater ist angekommen!

4.4 Nenne mich nicht einen Lügner! Ich habe die Königin in einem roten Bikini gesehen, als ich 15 Jahre alt war!

4.5 Über was zum Teufel sprichst du?!

4.6 Schau zum Himmel hinauf, so wirst du drei Drachen sehen, die gegeneinander kämpfen, wenn die Zeit gekommen ist.

4.7 Oh, mir war nicht bewusst, dass du das warst, der letzte Nacht im See schwamm.

4.8 Ich weiß, aber sei bitte von jetzt an vorsichtiger.

4.9 Bitte hole mir ein kühles Getränk. Ich bin durstig.

5. *Übung*

5.1 When did Linus leave the house?

5.2 Two hundred years ago, there was an eclipse of the sun.

5.3 The more I think, the more I get confused.

5.4 Get out of your bed, Linus!

5.5 Why have you scolded Saphira?

5.6 Aaaah, over there are five orcs!

6. Übung

6.1 There's no need to cast a new spell.

6.2 Is there an old book in 'Vinegar Castle'?

6.3 No, I didn't see a person wearing a green hat.

6.4 There are four old wise men: Irinas, Salaryna, Telarius, Sonorius.

6.5 The stars were sparkling while I was lying in the hammock.

6.6 Go to the Queen at once; it's urgent!

6.7 Can you see the throne of the Queen?

6.8 He said that he had seen you with Reinhard going to the marketplace.

7. Übung

7.1 angry, angrier, angriest

7.2 funny, funnier, funniest

7.3 large, larger, largest

7.4 small, smaller, smallest

7.5 great, greater, greatest

7.6 cold, colder, coldest

7.7 hot, hotter, hottest

7.8 soft, softer, softest

7.9 weak, weaker, weakest

7.10 powerful, more powerful, most powerful

7.11 clear, clearer, clearest

7.12 thick, thicker, thickest

8. Übung

8.1 who

8.2 when

8.3 how

8.4 what

8.5 how

9. Übung

9.1 She told him not to touch that bottle and that it contained a dangerous fluid.

9.2 He told him to dream on and that he wasn't as good as he was.

9.3 She told him not to go there ever again and that there were evil fairies in the forest at night.

9.4 He asked her if she would help him with that.

9.5 He said that he had never seen a talking hamster.

9.6 He said that Saphira would have learned those spells by the end of this week.

9.7 He said that it was ok for him, that he would be waiting for her, and told her not to be late.

9.8 She said that she had known him for many years.

9.9 He said if he didn't mind, he would call Saphira.

9.10 He agreed and said that that would help him a lot.

10. Übung

10.1 I've already learned ten new spells today.

10.2 Did you see all those many shooting stars yesterday, too?

10.3 I'd rather like a new robe.

10.4 I'll never tell you a secret again!

10.5 Indeed, I'm very experienced in this field of magic.

10.6 Pass me the glass of water, please.

10.7 I'm going to ask about the magic ring.

10.8 Very good; I only need one more ingredient!

11. *Übung*

11.1 builds

11.2 waters

11.3 wakes up

11.4 chases

11.5 laugh

11.6 catches

11.7 dreams

12. Übung

12.1 Saphira asked if he knew where her magic wand was.

12.2 Linus said that they were on a journey to find four magic crystals.

12.3 Reinhard said that he understood and wished him/her well.

12.4 The Queen told him/her to find information about the recent strange happenings.

12.5 Saphira said that a dragon was standing on the frozen lake.

12.6 Linus said that he was sorry and hadn't got more gold coins.

12.7 Saphira said that she loved reading books in the library.

12.8 Linus said that his favourite toothbrush wasn't at its usual place.

12.9 Reinhard said that it had been a beautiful evening the day before.

12.10 The Queen said that her new gloves had just arrived.

13. Übung

13.1 Obacht! Die Steine sind rutschig!

13.2 Diese Rüstung ist preiswert! Ich möchte sie kaufen!

13.3 Ich stimme zu. Ich werde hier bleiben und die übrigen Monster besiegen.

13.4 Ich glaube, ich habe mir meinen Arm gebrochen. Bitte helft mir!

13.5 Zwei Orks kontrollieren die Brücke!

14. Übung

14.1 Saphira is so cute when she smiles.

14.2 Saphira and Linus have to protect a farm against demons.

14.3 Saphira has already been in the Empire of Inias.

14.4 Linus surely will be reading a book of his favourite author by the fireplace this evening.

14.5 Three weeks have passed now, and we still haven't received a message from the Queen of the Elves …

15. Übung

15.1 strongly

15.2 hard

15.3 heavily

15.4 clearly

15.5 softly

15.6 urgently

16. Übung

16.1 to grant, granted, granted

16.2 to offer, offered, offered

16.3 to cleanse, cleansed, cleansed

16.4 to bare, bared, bared

16.5 to water, watered, watered

16.6 to pour, poured, poured

16.7 to rain, rained, rained

16.8 to proof, proofed, proofed

16.9 to rescue, rescued, rescued

16.10 to heal, healed, healed

16.11 to save, saved, saved

16.12 to bring, brought, brought

17. Übung

17.1 If I went there, I would meet you.

17.2 If you knew him, he would know you.

17.3 If there was a treasure, I would want it.

17.4 If I inserted this stone, the door would open!

17.5 If there was no more juice, I would ask Saphira to buy another bottle.

17.6 If Linus was not at home, Saphira would tell you.

17.7 If Saphira needed a new bottle, she would tell Linus.

18. Übung

18.1 Saphira didn't see a ghost while she was looking for a legendary spell role.

18.2 Saphira and Linus won't let the enemy capture their beloved town.

18.3 Linus is making a sandwich for himself.

18.4 Saphira is running across the meadow.

18.5 Linus had eaten the whole cake when Saphira came home.

18.6 Reinhard and the Queen are talking about a funny play that will be performed next Sunday.

18.7 Four bandits have just robbed a rich merchant.

18.8 Time flies, don't you think?

19. Übung

19.1 Wo bist du so lange gewesen?

19.2 Willkommen zuhause, meine liebe Schwester!

19.3 Nachdem Saphira ihre Arbeit im Laboratorium beendet hatte, ging sie mit Linus spazieren.

19.4 Kannst du dir vorstellen, wie brilliant jener Zauberer gewesen sein muss?

19.5 Ich habe noch nie von solch einer albernen Geschichte gehört!

19.6 Vielleicht werden wir uns wieder sehen ...

19.7 Der Tod wird uns nicht bekommen! Lass uns diesen Trank trinken und unsterblich werden!

19.8 Geh mir aus dem Weg! Wage es nicht, mir noch einmal über den Weg zu laufen!

20. Übung

20.1 Saphira wants to talk to Reinhard about a strange creature that she saw nearby the town.

20.2 Linus would like to dress the salad.

20.3 Saphira and Linus haven't seen Aunt Julica for 5 years.

20.4 What's so important about this spell?

20.5 Would you like to accompany us to the next tavern?